THE BOOK OF THE
Dragon

THE BOOK OF THE
Dragon

◆ CIRUELO ◆

STERLING
New York

STERLING
New York

An Imprint of Sterling Publishing
387 Park Avenue South
New York, NY 10016

The Book of the Dragon by Ciruelo
Spanish Edition published by Timun Mas, Spain 1991
English edition first published by Paper Tiger, Great Britain 1992
German edition, DAC Editions, Spain 2000
French edition, DAC Editions, Spain 2003
Italian edition, DAC Editions, Spain 2003

To contact DAC Editions:
www.dac-editions.com
ciruelo@dac-editions.com

This edition published by Sterling Publishing Co., Inc.,
by arrangement with H. G. Ciruelo Cabral

ISBN 978-1-4027-2811-2 (hardcover)
ISBN 978-1-4549-0119-8 (paperback)

Distributed in Canada by Sterling Publishing
c/o Canadian Manda Group, 165 Dufferin Street
Toronto, Ontario, Canada M6K 3H6
Distributed in the United Kingdom by GMC Distribution Services
Castle Place, 166 High Street, Lewes, East Sussex, England BN7 1XU
Distributed in Australia by Capricorn Link (Australia) Pty. Ltd.
P.O. Box 704, Windsor, NSW 2756, Australia

For information about custom editions, special sales, and premium and corporate purchases,
please contact Sterling Special Sales at 800-805-5489 or specialsales@sterlingpublishing.com.

Printed in China
All rights reserved

2 4 6 8 10 9 7 5 3 1

www.sterlingpublishing.com

Dedicated to all the extinct species.

Contents

Introduction
14

Part One
General Information
18

Part Two
Types of Dragons
38

Part Three
Culture and Customs
72

Part Four
Legends
90

Epilogue
138

Index
140

Introduction

Everybody knows what dragons are. They are enormous, fierce, bloodthirsty creatures appearing in fairy tales and legends primarily as accessories, functioning mainly to set off the bravery of the knights challenging them. Dragons are obscure, mysterious characters described only in broad terms, little more than foils to enhance a hero's valor. Dragons, though, are much more than this. They are intelligent and educated creatures who lead enthralling lives.

The Book of the Dragon was written after careful study of ancient manuscripts and patient following of the dragons' trail throughout the world. We hope to draw the reader into a world within our grasp, yet beyond it at the same time. In this book, you will find descriptions of dragons' habits, customs, and tastes, as well as a catalog of the different types of dragons, together with their physical attributes and modes of existence. You will also find ancient stories about dragons whose terrifying appearance inspired famous legends dealing with good and evil.

We do not, however, claim that this book is an encyclopedia of dragons or an exhaustive study on dragon science, for such work would fill volumes. We are simply allowing the reader to enter into the secret world of dragons, making this a useful book for anyone who admires and is interested in these beautiful beasts. Readers not acquainted with the charms and qualities of dragons can now discover, and learn to appreciate, these fascinating creatures.

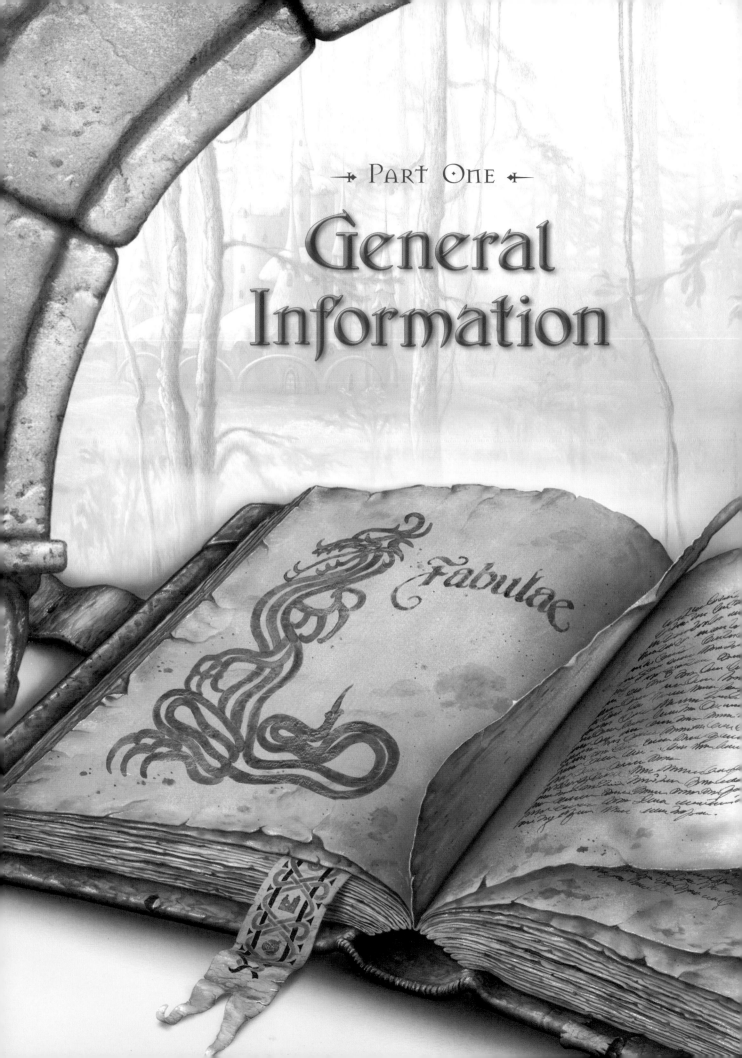

Part One
General Information

Fabulae

Psychological Characteristics

Adult dragons are astute, powerful, and sure of their strength. Their cunning helps them elude the ingenious traps laid by man, and their spirits could be described as playful. They are usually avaricious and fairly insolent, which is to be expected given their power and considerable physical strength. Dragons are very fond of jewels and precious stones, and they hoard treasure greedily. Perfect connoisseurs, they are discerning in their appreciation of gems, and it is not easy to deceive them as to the values of stones. They are lovers of conundrums, often promising to set their victims free on the condition that they find answers to riddles.

Dragons are usually very proud, and are acutely sensitive to ridicule. Nothing infuriates them

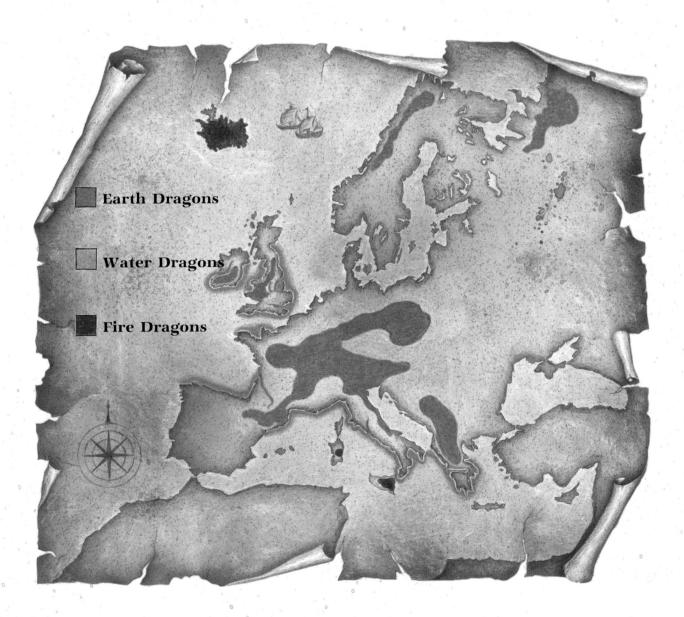

☐ **Earth Dragons**

☐ **Water Dragons**

◼ **Fire Dragons**

more than being made fun of by humans. This is something we have to bear in mind when dealing with dragons. If we embarrass them, they will refuse to have anything to do with us. If we speak to them circumspectly, however, and show that we are capable of keeping their secrets, we will gain their trust and achieve great influence over them.

Dragons are well-versed in magic, and understand the power associated with names. Dragons keep their names closely-guarded secrets; in fact, names are so important that the surest way to defeat and subdue dragons is to discover their names.

The true names of dragons synthesize their personalities and their histories. These names express dragons' origins and also all that dragons have achieved during their lives: their aspirations, their knowledge, and their levels of the mastery of magic. Their names are usually conferred on them at birth or at a young age, but they are modified throughout their lives. The secret is guarded so carefully that a dragon's real name is known only to the dragon himself and the Dragon Father. Dragons also have one or several assumed names by which they are known. We would like to emphasize that, out of

respect for dragon practice, all names used here are assumed names.

For easy reference, we have grouped dragons into three large families: Earth Dragons, Water Dragons, and Fire Dragons.

➡ Nuptial route taken by Water Dragons

⇨ Nuptial route taken by all other dragons

General Comments and Physiology

Dragons (*Drago drago*) are homoiothermic reptiles. In other words, they are warm-blooded creatures and their body temperatures are controlled internally; they are not dependent on the warmth from the sun like other reptiles.

This characteristic enables them to adapt to different climates of their extensive habitat, and maintain their activities both day and night throughout the year. Dragons generally have wings, and hollow bones so that they can remain light in the air. There are dragons—usually ancient survivors from the distant past—with stumpy legs and no wings. These rare survivors of a remote era are intelligent and fairly aggressive, and belong to a single species on the verge of extinction known as "worms of the deep." These creatures live for a very long time. There are records of dragons who have lived for five hundred and even a thousand years, but there are no known cases of dragons who have died from old age. Rather, dragons die from accidents, certain diseases, or as a result of the actions of their most relentless enemy: MAN.

Dragons are susceptible to few illnesses, and the most serious threats vary from one family to another. In the case of Fire Dragons, the worst disease is scale corrosion, which can be fatal. Senile dementia is more common among Earth

Dragons, while acute gastritis *non virginae* affects mainly the Water Dragons, which have extremely delicate stomachs.

Despite their strength, dragons lose some of their agility with age, easily falling prey to the singular and terrible dragon-killer, the armor-plated *Ichneumon*. This swamp dweller, which Pliny describes in his *Historia Naturalis* as a spindle-shaped mud fish with a sharp snout covered with tough plates, is the dragon's mortal enemy. The *Ichneumon* burrows between the dragon's scales, and using its sharp snout, tunnels through the tender flesh until it reaches the entrails, devouring them and killing its victim.

Dragons can talk, and they speak in Latin, a tongue that is innate in the dragon species. They have no difficulty, however, in learning and expressing themselves correctly in the vernacular of the region in which they live.

Lovers of woodlands and fresh air, dragons cannot bear environmental pollution or the tumult of civilization. The only exception to this rule is one particular subspecies of Fire Dragons—*Draco flamula*—which we will explain later. Today dragons survive only in rare places that have escaped pollution—those small isolated pockets of the Old World where the future of dragons seems precarious.

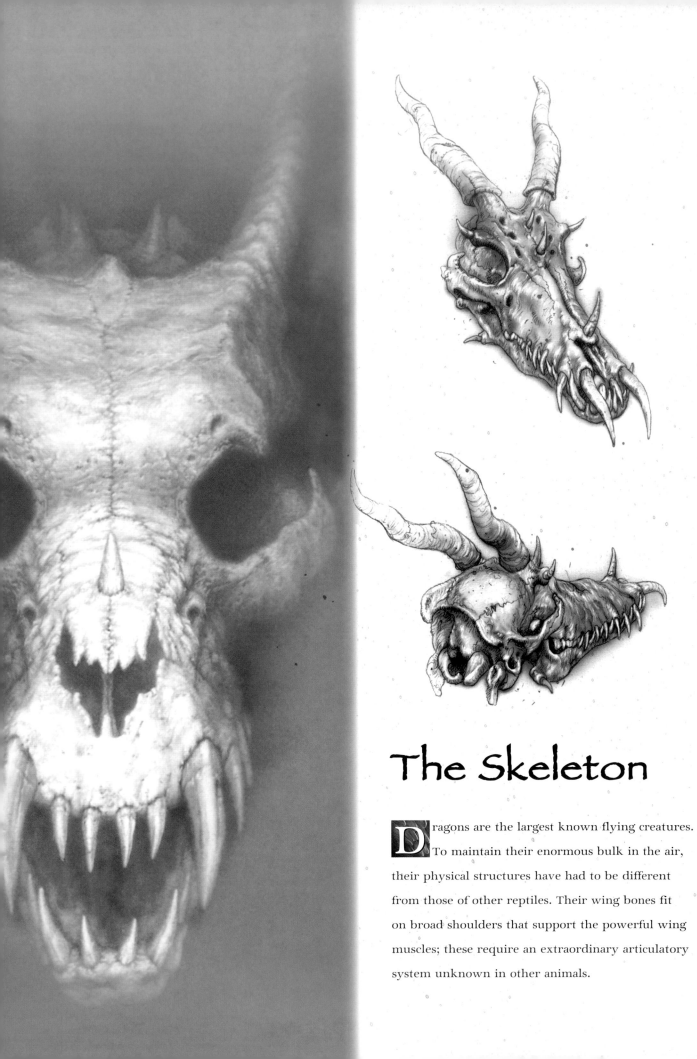

The Skeleton

Dragons are the largest known flying creatures. To maintain their enormous bulk in the air, their physical structures have had to be different from those of other reptiles. Their wing bones fit on broad shoulders that support the powerful wing muscles; these require an extraordinary articulatory system unknown in other animals.

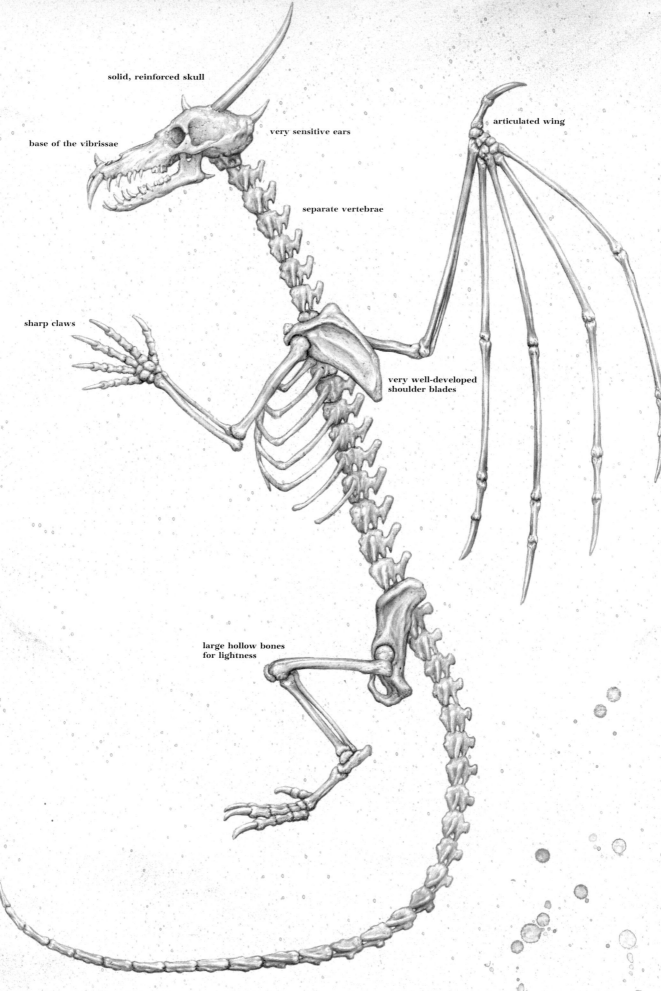

solid, reinforced skull

base of the vibrissae

very sensitive ears

separate vertebrae

articulated wing

sharp claws

very well-developed
shoulder blades

large hollow bones
for lightness

25

There are some dragons who are experts in black magic and employed in the service of evil. They use their powers to bewitch dragon servants who, even after the dragon's death, guard the dragon's abundant hoards of treasure. These terrible creatures practice black magic and are very difficult to thwart without the help of a very learned wizard.

The Scales

Dragons' bodies are completely covered with tough, shiny scales. The only exceptions are Earth Dragons, who do not have this scaly armor on their necks or stomachs, possibly due to their habit of burrowing underground. These dragons often wear jeweled breastplates to protect their soft abdomens. Using their saliva, which has powerful adhesive properties and is secreted on an empty stomach, Earth Dragons stick precious stones onto their necks and stomachs. This is for protection as well as adornment. The scales are shaped like pentagonal teardrops, with two long sides and two shorter ones, and a very short fifth side attached to the skin.

Dragons can make their scales stand on end whenever they preen themselves. Remember: dragons are very clean creatures and always take great care to keep their skin and scales immaculate. In their normal position, the scales overlap neatly, and, thanks to a tiny cavity on the surface, fit into each other to allow perfect freedom of movement.

If we could study a scale closely, we would notice the innermost part is composed of a compact hairy formation firmly rooted in the epidermis. On each hair follicle, there are some tiny glands that secrete a substance that adheres firmly to the skin. This substance is rich in minerals, which determine the hardness and color of the dragons' scales. The external surface has a horned, translucent texture that gives the scales their habitual luster.

Dragons do not need to slough off their skin like most other reptiles, since the scales grow and are renewed automatically just like human nails and hair. They are not shed from the body, except in cases of illness.

Cross Section

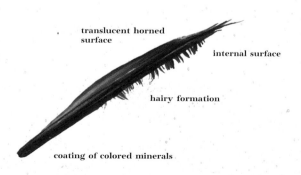

translucent horned surface

internal surface

hairy formation

coating of colored minerals

Frontal Section

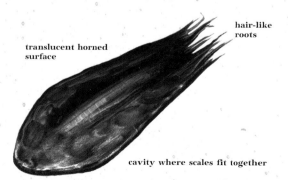

hair-like roots

translucent horned surface

cavity where scales fit together

27

Scales of Armor

The mercenary warrior who hired himself out to towns and sovereigns to slay dragons usually wore a suit of armor made from dragon scales. This garment gave him enormous prestige and proclaimed to all that he had slain one of these fearsome beasts. Incidentally, the scales on his armor are very small, a clear indication that the dragon he killed was a young one who had barely reached puberty—hence much easier to vanquish than an adult.

Coloring

It is impossible to list the enormous variety of hues that make up the dragon's brilliant coloring, but they can be divided into three broad color groupings:

Blues: ranging from mother-of-pearl and silver to dark blue

Reds: ranging from copper red to dark red and reddish-black

Greens: including every imaginable shade of green, yellow, dark brown, emerald green, and burnished gold

Although these three principal color groups usually are not mixed, a dragon's coloring is rarely uniform. In general, its scales are several hues from one of the main color categories, with a metallic luster that is hard to define. When the scales have a pale, opaque appearance, it is a sure sign of ill health. Many dragons arc known by the predominant colors of their scales, such as Ancalagon the Black, Smaug the Golden, and Spars the Green.

The Dragon's Abode

Dragons usually live in natural caves and caverns that they adapt to their needs. The dragon's abode consists of two or more rooms, but the room closest to the entrance always retains its original purpose: to divert the suspicions of curious human beings. Normally, this entrance is concealed by plants and rocks and is just big enough to allow the creatures to go in and out. Over the years, the continual friction of the dragon's scaly body against the cave walls makes the walls smooth and polished. Dragons choose caves that are big enough for them to turn around in if they are pursued, but not big enough to conceal enemies.

The process of finding a home is always the same: the dragon emits an ultrasound vibration, and the sensitive *vibrissae*, or "cat's whiskers," around the mouth capture the echo, enabling the dragon to locate the grottoes in the vicinity. The dragon looks for two adjacent caves, and once it has identified the ones it wants, it digs passages the exact width of its body to connect the two caves. The dragon enlarges and polishes its inner cave with great care, checks that there are no kinks or ways out, and plugs any

holes. Then it makes, or gets servants to make, a small ventilation hole. As the dragon requires more space, it digs out new rooms until it has created cave complexes where it can live comfortably with enough room for its servants and treasures.

This is the most common type of dwelling among Earth Dragons and Water Dragons. Fire Dragons have a different social structure and some very different habits and customs. In the chapters devoted to each species, we will give more detailed descriptions of different abodes and the servants associated with each family.

The Dragon Father

ragon families are organized into hierarchical societies that revolve around the figure of a wise and judicious male: the head of the family, known as the Dragon Father or Dragon King. All other dragons pledge obedience to him. It is his task to make peace and adjudicate when there are family quarrels or territorial disputes, and to confer a secret name on each of his subjects.

This ancient male usually exercises his privileges with moderation. His Council is made up of an unspecified number of young dragons who act as his bodyguards and pages. There are also virgin dragonesses who have not reached the required maturity to mate. It is the Dragon Father who decides when the females are ready for mating. He is assisted by the elder female dragons who are no longer fertile and have withdrawn from wandering the world. These dragonesses, who are well-versed in magic, are given the honorary titles of Queen and hold full authority in the Council. It is left to the Queens to choose the successor to the Dragon Father at the time of his death.

Dragonesses

Female dragons are very scarce, so they are treated with special reverence. Therefore when rare female eggs—recognized by their darker color—are laid, they are treated with the utmost care and attention. Male dragons will cautiously incubate these precious eggs, keeping close watch and turning them over gently from time to time.

When it is time for the eggs to hatch, the anxious fathers take them to safe places, far from human settlements, and build nests well concealed from prying eyes. As soon as the baby dragonesses emerge from their shells, the fathers bring them food so they can eat without venturing out of their nests.

When the baby dragonesses are strong enough to hold on to their fathers' shoulders, their fathers whisk them through the air to the dragon Council. Here they will live with the rest of the young females, until the Dragon Father considers them mature enough to mate.

As a result of being protected and raised by the group, the physical development of the young females is faster than that of the males; they also reach sexual maturity more rapidly. It is not unusual for them to start talking before the wing sacs have disappeared. Dragonesses command great respect and reverence. Often prouder and fiercer than males, they are very protective of their privileges.

By the time dragonesses are ready for their first mating flights, they have become beautiful adult beasts and have received intensive instruction in all fields of dragon knowledge. They set out on these flights alone, but are joined by the males who wish to mate with them. Eventually a single female ends up in the center of a flight of adult male dragons. These flights—which can easily be spotted due to their sheer size—travel toward a destination chosen by the Dragon Father for the union.

Young dragonesses, who are expert magicians, sometimes change themselves into women of great beauty. They are able to sustain these illusory personalities longer than males. Dragonesses have been known to enter human society without revealing their true identities and preserve their human forms for considerable lengths of time.

Favorites

The rarity of dragonesses is another powerful influence on the social organization of the species, and on the dragon's capacity for forming emotional attachments.

Dragons mate only six or seven times in their lifetimes, if they are lucky. The males can only stay with the females for a few hours, so they do not become attached to their temporary mates. While dragons, as intelligent beings, need social and physical contact, they are unsociable by nature and profoundly competitive, seeing other dragons as potential rivals. This makes it impossible for them to form friendships with other dragons.

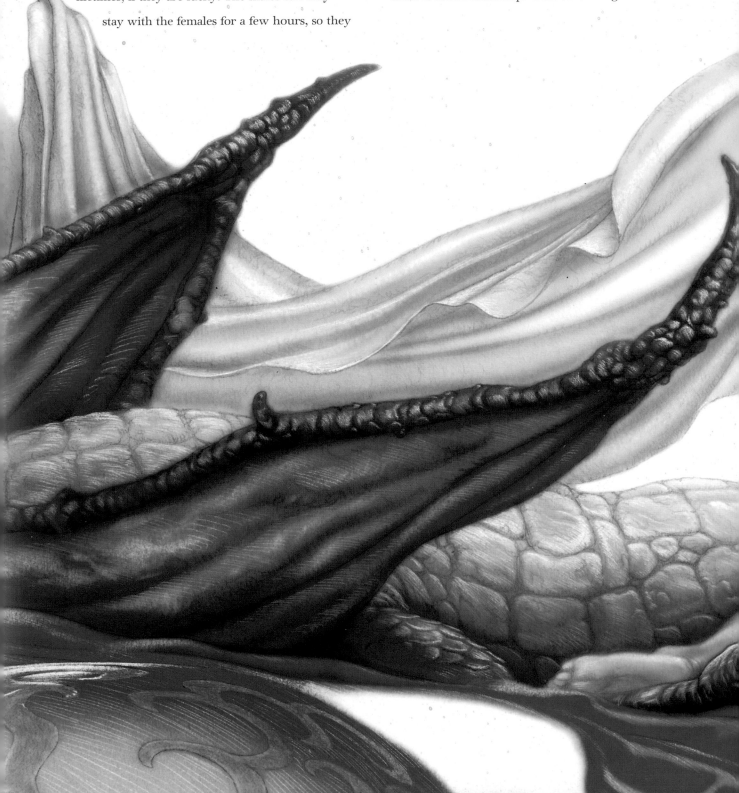

This frustration is the reason why dragons fulfill their need for affection by keeping "favorites," usually human servants kept almost as companions. Pampered and spoiled by their dragon masters, the favorites usually sleep with them; their only obligations are to caress them, sing to them, and accompany them whenever they wish.

Dragons capriciously choose new favorites; when they do so, they usually release the old ones in order to avoid problems of jealousy.

Favorites should not be confused with dragons' ladies. These are women with whom dragons usually forge strong and lasting relationships.

❖ Part Two ❖
Types of Dragons

Fabulae

The Great Earth Dragon

The most common and abundant dragon species found on our planet is that of *Draco rex Cristatus*, or Great Earth Dragon, as it is commonly called.

They are great winged creatures of enormous size. They can grow from fifty to one hundred feet in length, and have a full wing span of up to one hundred feet.

Their coloring is usually green-brown, with their many-hued scales ranging from lemon yellow to emerald green. There are some Earth Dragons who can breathe fire, although the force of their flames is not as powerful as that of Fire Dragons.

Earth Dragons are expert fliers and gliders. Although their great size sometimes makes take-off awkward, once in the air they can reach great altitudes, and cover enormous distances by gliding solely on wind currents.

Draco rex are introverts and reserved by nature. They do not like being around members of their own species other than in the mating season, and even then only for a limited time.

Given the size and strength of these particular dragons, squabbles can be dangerous. Interestingly though, when Earth Dragons grow old, it is not unusual for them to be accompanied by young pages. The Earth Dragons will instruct them in dragon wisdom, and the fortunate pages will usually inherit all their wealth.

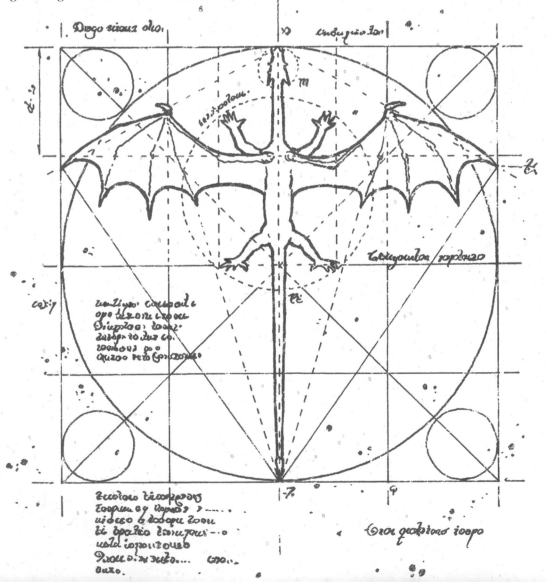

The Egg

Earth Dragons mate only during the very
rare rainy seasons when a particular flower is
blooming in the African and Asian deserts. On
these occasions, the males congregate around
one female who sets off on her nuptial flight.
Although the females are always bigger than the
males, they are extremely agile in the air.

When a female soars up into the air, the males
ecstatically pursue her in a ballet of graceful, aerial
acrobatics. The most agile dragon eventually catches
up with her. He waits for the moment when the
female unfolds her wings to their maximum span,
and then their union takes place at a great height.

The male slides under the belly of his beloved and enfolds her in a close embrace of wings and talons. Thus entwined, the pair reach their climax while plunging rapidly down to the ground. Only when they are a few yards from the ground do they part and spread their wings to land.

After their nuptial flight, the couple withdraws to the heart of the desert. There, the female makes a nest in the warm, damp sand, and lays a single egg about the size of an ostrich egg. If the egg is male, it is mottled green and gray, while a female egg is slightly darker. Once the dragoness has built the nest and laid the egg, she flies away, leaving the male to incubate the egg.

Dragonesses make several ritual nuptial flights during the mating season. From all these unions, however, only two or three females will be born. When the baby dragon has hatched, the doting father takes it to a suitable place for a young dragon, usually in temperate forests, where it is easy to find food.

The dragon leaves his young as soon as he has found a safe place, and never hunts in the nearby area, so as not to reveal the hiding place. He continues to keep watch over the area, however, flying back and forth at a great height to avoid being seen.

The Young

Baby Earth Dragons might easily be mistaken for large lizards, like the spotted lizard, which is very common in some parts of the world. Newly-hatched dragons measure some twenty-four inches in length, and their wings—encased in sacs—look at first glance like typical lizard markings.

Baby dragons' tails are not segmented; if caught, they are not able to shed them like other reptiles. Thanks to their relatively large size and tremendous agility, baby dragons are able to elude predators such as foxes, badgers, and birds of prey that would otherwise devour them.

At about eight or nine months, they are the size of large dogs, now able to tackle animals as

large and fierce as wolves. They hunt and eat foxes and mountain goats, as well as stray sheep and calves, but always in moderation to avoid discovery by humans. This behavior is instinctive in young dragons, whose intelligence has not yet developed. Their nocturnal habits, their caution, and their extreme timidity make it very difficult to observe young dragons during this period.

When dragons enter adolescence, at around the age of two, the fathers cease their vigilance and the young dragons are gradually left to their own devices. The adolescent dragon has already attained a considerable size, which makes camouflage difficult. At about this time, their wings begin to

unfold and their intelligence becomes more acute as the proverbial cunning of the species starts to manifest itself.

As their innate knowledge of Latin develops, they also learn the dialect of the region where they live. The young dragons begin to hunt, devouring everything they come across, from flocks of sheep to men and women. In the early years, adolescent dragons are usually proud fighters, with little inclination toward poetry and magic, which is how they can wreak the greatest havoc.

Young dragons have no fixed abodes, and they are not in the service of other dragons. They have developed a love of jewels and have started to collect precious stones, used as beds and as breastplates for their soft bellies. They feel the urge to accumulate wealth.

When they reach the age of four, the young dragons fly to the Council of the Dragon Father. Here they will live for a couple of years to learn social customs and be initiated into the art of magic. When this period is over, they receive their secret names. Now they are ready to settle down, either independently or as dragon pages to adult males who will take them under their tutelage. During this period, they are not ready to reproduce.

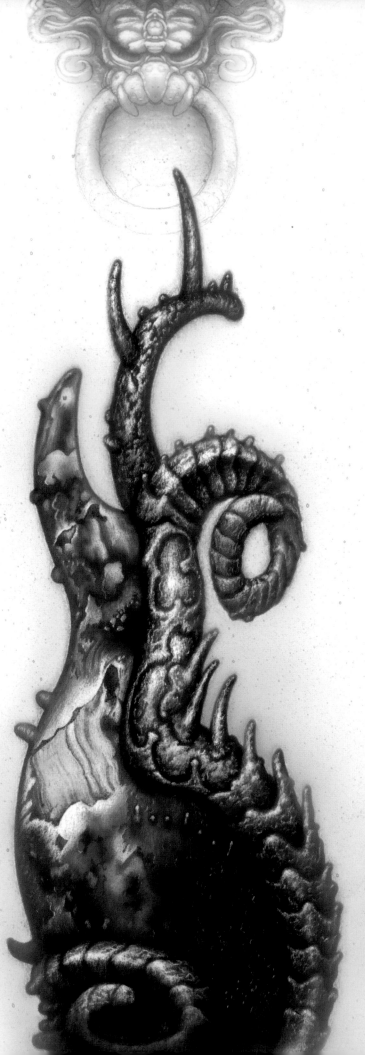

Social Organization

If we were to enter the spacious cave complex of an Earth Dragon's abode, we would first come across a crudely excavated entrance. From here a narrow corridor with high, polished walls leads to the inner cave. The bedroom usually composes the central cave, where the treasure that serves as the dragon's bed is carefully arranged. This room—considered the principal quarter—is always kept clean and tidy. It is often adorned with beautiful and rare objects, tastefully arranged by the servants. These include luminous mosses, strangely shaped roots and stones, sculptures, and artifacts of gold and silverwork— the spoils from the dragon's lootings. The servants' bedrooms are usually located behind the main room. There is yet another cave beyond, which is much smaller, where the dragon pages have their own sleeping quarters.

The common belief that dragons are dirty and unkempt and that their homes are full of leftover food is completely unfounded. Like all animals that live in caves and burrows, dragons like to maintain clean and tidy homes. But here, it is the servants' job to carry out these domestic duties.

The Earth Dragon's servants are gnomes, elves, other woodland creatures, and human beings. Some are captured by the dragon itself, and others are acquired through exchanges with other dragons. The servants' duties include cleaning and arranging the home, as well as brushing and cleaning their master's scales. They also keep them company. Servants do not lead wretched lives, as might be expected; their dragon master is not generally cruel to them, but rather treats them with kindness and generosity.

The notion that Earth Dragons eat their servants when they are old and have outlived their usefulness is utterly false. In fact, this has only happened on two occasions. In both cases, the dragon in question was very old and suffering from senile dementia, a brain-wasting disease that sometimes affects this dragon species due

to the enormous quantities of meats and fats it consumes.

More commonly, close friendships develop between Earth Dragons and their servants, and the servants accompany their master to the amazing fire festivals held every five years at the court of the Dragon Father.

We must remember that Earth Dragons do not build up relationships with other members of their species very easily. These dragons show a special preference for young servants with beautiful singing voices, as we know every dragon's love of music is legendary. A girl servant with these attributes can become a male dragon's favorite; he will sleep with his head on her soft lap and adorn his beloved with jewels when he presents her to the Council of the Dragon Father. This wise father is very tolerant toward his subjects' whims.

Much has been written about dragons who have offered friendship to their servants; there are instances of profound and genuine affection between many a dragon and human being.

Water Dragons

Water Dragons, or *Draco splendens*, are rarer than Earth Dragons. They can be found in both salt and fresh water, but above all they prefer lakes.

Magnificently colored, these beasts are perfectly at home in water, moving through it with great agility and speed. Although their front legs end in sharp claws, their back legs have been transformed into fins, hampering their movements on land. They have tremendous lung capacity and can store oxygen in their stomachs and transfer it to the lungs when they need it, enabling them to remain underwater for hours on end. Because they live in water, these dragons have partially lost the ability to fly, and can make only short gliding flights—although some of them can attain a reasonable air speed.

Water Dragons have very specific eating habits—especially the adults—which is why the few remaining individuals are in danger of extinction. Apparently, Water Dragons only eat human virgins. If this requirement is not satisfied, as is often the case, legend has it that these beasts suffer excruciating indigestion, which leaves them at death's door. The only cure considered effective is massive doses of almond oil and a concoction made from orange blossom and magnolia petals.

Water Dragons are physically much more beautiful and graceful than Earth Dragons. They have soft, melodic voices and cherish beauty above all else. They are inspired poets and can spend hours contemplating their own reflections in water, in narcissistic poses, or they can become ecstatic over a beautiful sunset. There are stories of dragons who have rejected the maidens they were about to eat because they were not beautiful or not correctly attired. The fact is, they love their victims to be dressed in sumptuous silks, with circlets of fresh flowers in their hair. Water Dragons are also amorous creatures; there have been several occasions when the maiden destined for supper has become the queen of the dragon's heart.

They are brave adversaries, and if called upon to fight, they will defend themselves ferociously to the death. They tend to be timid, however, and it is not possible to catch more than a glimpse of them at twilight. They always conduct themselves with elegance and grace.

The behavior of *Draco splendens* is very different from *Draco rex Cristatus*. One curious fact is that these delicate and beautiful water creatures cannot bear any kind of chains or bonds around their necks. For this reason, in antiquity it

was sufficient to tie a noose of eglantine around their necks to capture them; thus tied, they would allow themselves to be led away without a struggle. Many

Water Dragons were captured in this way, the dragon of Mont Blanc, the Tarasque, and the dragons of Sant Mer de Banyoles and of Llac Negre among them.

Sea Serpent Dragons

Water Dragons have often been sighted throughout history, particularly by mariners on their long voyages around the vast oceans of the world. During the conquest of the New World, varied reports circulated about huge creatures that had been sighted in the ocean. These descriptions all dealt with dragons that can now be recognized as part of the same species.

The last reported sighting, dating back to the nineteenth century, comes from Peter Karl van Esling, the director of the Hague Zoo. He gave an account of a Water Dragon seen during a voyage to collect marine species in the Atlantic in 1860:

We were sailing west through a calm sea as the day was coming to its close when suddenly we saw what seemed to be a gigantic type of reptile, covered with brilliant blue and sparkling silver scales.

The massive hulk appeared to swim gracefully around the ship before our incredulous eyes, writhed and turned three times and then submerged itself without so much as a splash—and hardly a ripple—as it plunged back down to the deeps.

We had enough time to see that its eyes were horribly livid and enormous, yet these eyes and the vertical yellow slits for its pupils seemed to show an uncommon intelligent expression, though very fierce. They seemed to be luminous, but this effect could simply have been due to the reflections from the last rays of the setting sun. Its head was adorned with the brightest azure and emerald crests.

Even though it disappeared under water so quickly and we did not see it again, we all agreed it measured something approaching seven meters [twenty-three feet] in length.

On its back too we could make out something resembling crests or fins, but the sailor beside me thought he saw legs and claws. It was basically serpentine of titanic proportions—quite unlike any other marine creature any of us had ever set eyes upon.

We baptized it Megophias.

Mating and the Young

We know about the life cycle of *Draco splendens*, thanks to the investigations of the eminent English botanist and explorer Sir Reginald Wort. At the close of the eighteenth century, he spent months observing the fauna of the Sargasso Sea. In the course of his investigations into Water Dragons, the British aristocrat witnessed their nuptial ceremonies.

His patient observations have given us the following account:

The female looks for a seaweed-covered bed on which she lies and emits a luminescent glow. Her brilliant colors cause the males to launch into an energetic display of acrobatics. They leap into the air only to disappear again into the sea, resembling streaks of colored light.

The female being courted then swims rapidly down to the depths of the ocean, followed by the throng of males. Only the fastest and strongest succeed in mating with her. After mating has taken place the female dragon hands over the fertilized egg to her partner. He deposits it in the warm sands of a safe beach and watches over it until it hatches. When the young dragon is born the father's duty is done and he disappears. By leaving, he does not betray the young dragon's presence to predators. During his lonely infancy, the young dragon feeds on tropical fruits and is strictly vegetarian.

Sir Reginald was wrong, however, on one point. The little dragon is not abandoned, as would appear from casual observation. The father visits his young at night, watching over the area from a prudent distance during the day. The truth of this is borne out by the dramatic fate which befell a bold but inexperienced naturalist. This was told in the *Diary of Expeditions and Discoveries of the New World* by the Portuguese adventurer Da Silva, in 1612:

Paulo and the young André Do Gao disembarked on the lush island, which seemed to be inhabited only by birds and crabs. Paulo saw a

huge brilliantly colored water lizard which appeared to be quite tame but very timid. He called his companion and they managed to catch the creature.

When the two naturalists wanted to bring it on board their ship, the beast let out a series of shrill cries. Immediately from the sea appeared an enormous lizard which threw itself on the unfortunate pair. André died in the fray with his head virtually torn from his body. Paulo managed to survive because he threw the basket with the young lizard back into the sea. Immediately the sea monster abandoned the pursuit to save the drowning beast.

We were so overwhelmed by this incident that we did not dare return to the island to recover André's body and bury him.

This little-known tale was considered spurious in scientific circles at the time, but it confirms our studies of the behavior of *Draco splendens*.

The Development of *Draco Splendens*

When the young *Draco splendens* has grown over three feet, its coloring becomes brighter and more luminous. It loves the water and soon starts to paddle around. When the father believes the young dragon is able to swim, it abandons the youth once and for all. Then the young dragon continues its adult life elsewhere.

During their first days by themselves, young Water Dragons often howl pitifully, but they soon get used to being alone. Their instincts prompt them to take to the water, leaving the land forever. During this phase, they feed solely on sea anemones, which do not harm them, even though they are poisonous. After a while, all young Water Dragons follow the Gulf Stream, setting off in search of places to make their permanent homes.

During these journeys, they reach full maturity. By the time the dragons reach the European shores, they are magnificent creatures measuring twenty-three feet in length, brilliantly colored and beautiful to behold. They have also mastered the power of speech and have become expert magicians.

Carried by subterranean currents unknown to man, they penetrate the European mainland. *Draco splendens* cannot tolerate polluted water, and eat only once a month, feasting on virgins.

The Water Dragon's Abode

The usual home of *Draco splendens* is a cave with a submerged entrance. Curiously, this cave is always dry, the floor being covered with sand that the dragon itself brings from the beach. This complex of caverns is bigger and more elaborately fashioned than that of the Earth Dragon. The rooms are decorated with pearls, corals, and gems of great beauty, which the dragon has collected over the years. With these, the dragon creates original and elaborate patterns. Stalactites and stalagmites are also part of the decor of the cave, while artistically arranged vases of flowers enhance the rooms.

It is not unusual for there to be a subterranean stream running through its cave. The dragon swims in it, and its servants drink the water and bathe in it.

A Water Dragon's family is small but select, and is usually made up of water creatures: lower-class water sprites with limited magic powers, small newts, and even a few human beings. Dragons cannot often capture water nymphs or sprites from large rivers, for these creatures are too wily. Among the human beings are poets and troubadours, and, very often, the maidens of the dragon's dreams.

The dragons' ladies are both their mistresses and their servants. *Draco splendens* lives luxuriously surrounded by a select entourage of damsels, pages, and squires. The taste these dragons have for art and their exclusive feeding habits mean their families have frequent contact with the outside world.

Fire Dragons

The rarest of the three species is the Fire Dragon, *Draco flameus*. It is extremely difficult to observe and study these dragons, since their habitat is inaccessible to human beings. These virtually unknown dragons live inside active volcanoes, and their natural surroundings are the great rivers of lava and fiery caverns in the belly of the Earth.

In this world of fire and incandescent molten rock dwells the Dragon Father. This is where courtship and mating take place. Here, too, rituals that no human being has ever witnessed are performed. Fire Dragons spend their infancies in these suffocating surroundings, only venturing outside when reaching maturity and only for brief hunting expeditions. Nocturnal creatures, Fire Dragons usually sally forth enveloped in flames when darkness reigns, but only if the weather is very dry and the sky clear. Water and humidity are a great threat to these creatures since they can cause scale corrosion—a fatal, painful disease for *Draco flameus*. This most horrible disease causes the scales to flake off from the body, leaving the dragon's sensitive skin exposed and vulnerable. This exposure not only causes dreadful burns produced by red-hot lava, but also total dehydration.

On their excursions into the outside world, Fire Dragons set vast expanses of land aflame. Scorching everything in their path, they avidly devour the charred remains of any animals left in the ashes. The dragon's mouth breathes fire, which is formed from a mixture of phosphorus and methane produced and stored in a second stomach. The mixture ignites on contact with oxygen immediately after it leaves the dragon's mouth.

The Fire Dragon's favorite food is composed of hydrocarbons—such as oil and bitumen—which it consumes in huge quantities. They also use these substances to clean and shine their scaly armor, an occupation to which Fire Dragons devote many hours. They take great care of every single scale and are always on the lookout for any suspicious-looking blemishes. This is not a question of vanity, even though dragons are very conceited creatures. This is because they need to guard against their most deadly enemy: the dreaded scale corrosion, mentioned earlier.

The scales, which cover the dragon's entire body, are made up of a type of metal and asbestos alloy. They are varicolored, ranging from bright golden yellow to red, copper, and black. These iridescent scales are the dragon's only protection against fire. Without this armor, the dragon is as susceptible to heat as any other living creature.

It has been reported that dragons of this species used to be abundant in the volcanoes of Iceland. They venture as far as Ireland and the north of Britain. In Italy a small colony of this charming species has survived in Sicily. Curiously, however, in Vesuvius there is no evidence whatsoever of the existence of *Draco flameus*.

These mysterious but fascinating beasts have large families of servants made up mainly of salamanders, will-o'-the-wisps, and other igneous creatures.

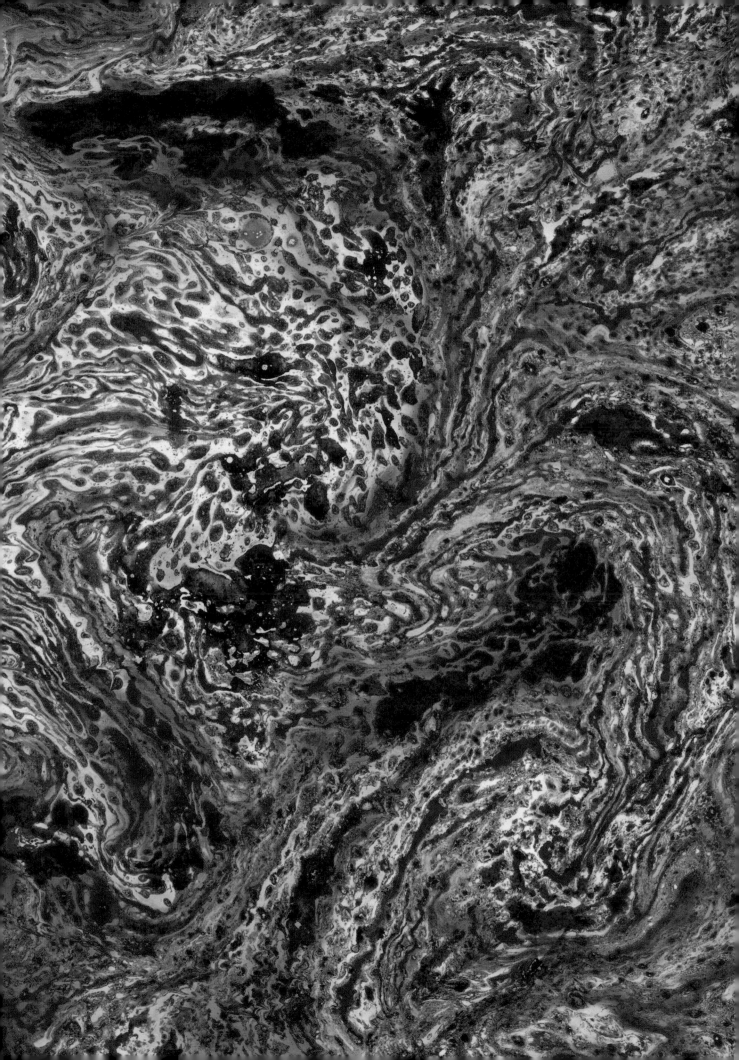

Social Organization

As stated earlier, Fire Dragons live in vast labyrinths of caves inside craters, among streams of lava and suffocating gases. Despite their strange and fearsome habitat, these are the most amicable and peace-loving of the great dragon races; they are also the most gregarious and outgoing. Fire Dragon society is organized into three large matriarchal groups. Powerful and sexually mature dragonesses occupy the principal caves of these colonies, and colonies under each of these Queens include several families of males and their sons. As is usual with all dragons, only paternity is recognized. The young are not considered descendants of the female but rather of the male. Consequently, Dragon Queens do not object to males joining their colonies with eggs from other dragonesses.

Within this matriarchal structure, a Dragon Father governs each individual family—but in the case of Fire Dragons, the hierarchy is not so rigid. Given that their habitat is restricted, the colonies are very close to each other and linked by narrow corridors. Dragons of the same age and sex live together, play together, and learn together. This close cohabitation with other members of their families means that Fire Dragons have the least contact with human beings. This is because they can satisfy their emotional needs among their own kind, either in couples or through friendship with their neighbors in the colony. They usually practice many group activities, although they always hunt alone so as not to frighten off prey.

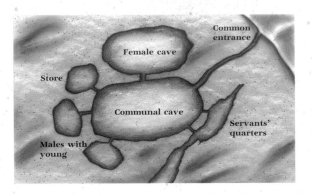

Little Fire Dragons

Draco flamula, usually under seven feet in length, is a subspecies of the Fire Dragon as it has evolved in modern times. The Little Fire Dragon lives in the chimneys of power stations, having adapted perfectly to the high temperatures and the concentrations of sulfur and sulfuric acid. Its scales have also taken on the sulfur-yellow and rust tones that facilitate camouflage, making it almost impossible to distinguish the dragon.

The first human being to see and identify this subspecies was an engineer and dragon enthusiast in a Bavarian power station. He gave it the name of *Flamula*, owing to the little tongue of flickering flame the dragon produces when he emerges from the chimney.

This subspecies is powerful and destructive, because when these creatures fly, they leave a trail of sulfurous gases. As we know, this produces acid rain, a phenomenon which destroys trees and damages vast areas of woodland all over the world. Some scholars believe Little Fire Dragons are a throwback of the dragon race, rather than an evolution of the species adapted to new surroundings. This theory seems to be borne from the loss of Latin as their principal language, as well as their lack of knowledge in any other language. This is also indicated by the absence of a stable social organization. It seems the other species of dragons despise and loathe their lowly diminutive relative.

Pirofagus Reptilis Catalanae

Another subspecies of the Fire Dragon is *Reptilis Catalanae*, which is very rare indeed, found only in the craters of Mount Etna in Sicily. Local inhabitants claim they were brought over by the Catalan conquistadors in the Middle Ages.

These creatures, with their dull, lusterless colors and short legs, were described at the beginning of the twentieth century by Professor Peter Ameisenhaufen. He classified them *Pirofagus reptilis Catalanae*. This name was given due to their presumed origin, but it is highly dubious, as far as we can see. They breathe fire like all Fire Dragons, but on inhaling they also breathe in their own flames, causing painful burns in the esophagus. They have to drink enormous quantities of water to soothe themselves. They lack the dragon's traditional faculty of speech, which seems to point to a very limited intelligence indeed. In his work *Fauna Secreta*, Professor Ameisenhaufen branded this unendearing creature an "accident of evolution."

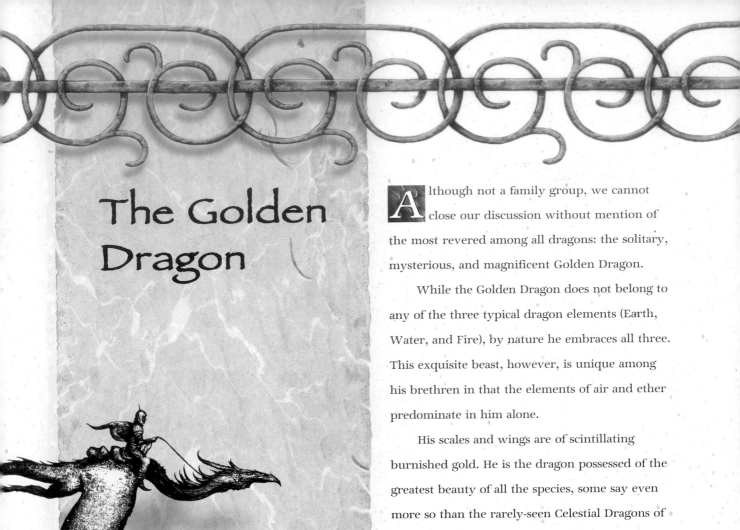

The Golden Dragon

Although not a family group, we cannot close our discussion without mention of the most revered among all dragons: the solitary, mysterious, and magnificent Golden Dragon.

While the Golden Dragon does not belong to any of the three typical dragon elements (Earth, Water, and Fire), by nature he embraces all three. This exquisite beast, however, is unique among his brethren in that the elements of air and ether predominate in him alone.

His scales and wings are of scintillating burnished gold. He is the dragon possessed of the greatest beauty of all the species, some say even more so than the rarely-seen Celestial Dragons of ancient Chinese legend. It is said that only three knights have set eyes upon the Golden Dragon, and only one single man has ever been his friend.

To understand something of this mysterious creature, we need to refer to the sparse information handed down to us from the supposedly original *Book of the Golden Dragon*, one of the secret books of dragon culture.

Tradition says that the Golden Dragon has never taken part in any aggressive action whatsoever. He is pure and unsullied by any flaw. He has also been known as the Keeper, and defends an enchanted castle where a pure-hearted knight devotedly helps him guard what is known as the Sacred Chalice.

This Sacred Chalice is said to be the hidden font and quintessence of the wisdom encompassed by a double principal: Life's secret lies in Comprehension rather than only in Knowledge. Its subtle, supernal messages have to be concealed from the minds of humans because they are not yet ready for them. Only three knights have ever succeeded in realizing some of its messages, and only one, who was free from stain, became its true custodian.

Thus, before the astonished gaze of his two companions, this pure-hearted knight and the Sacred Chalice were transported away by the Golden Dragon, with the promise that they would return to the outside world when the dwellers of this world were worthy of the chalice. The Golden Dragon carried the Guardian Knight to a crystal castle, in the heart of a hidden oak-wood, and is watching over the Guardian Knight until the illumination of the Sacred Chalice can be accepted on Earth. It is prophesied that when that happens, every single dragon will take flight to meet the Golden Dragon, carrying on their backs the chosen men who finally solved the enigmas of the chalice. The prophecy states that once humankind is properly enlightened, humans will eventually pay homage to the Guardian Knight of the Sacred Chalice and to the Golden Dragon.

It is said that through this eventual revelation, all nature will be cured of its terrible wounds. Fear and hatred will be purged. Peace will gradually break out instead of war, and a dawn emitted from the Sacred Chalice will bathe our weary world in golden light.

This myth, of course, has much in common with the legend of the Holy Grail and of Sir Galahad, which seems to indicate that dragons and poets were cast in very much the same mold. It also indicates that the Holy Grail and the knights really do exist.

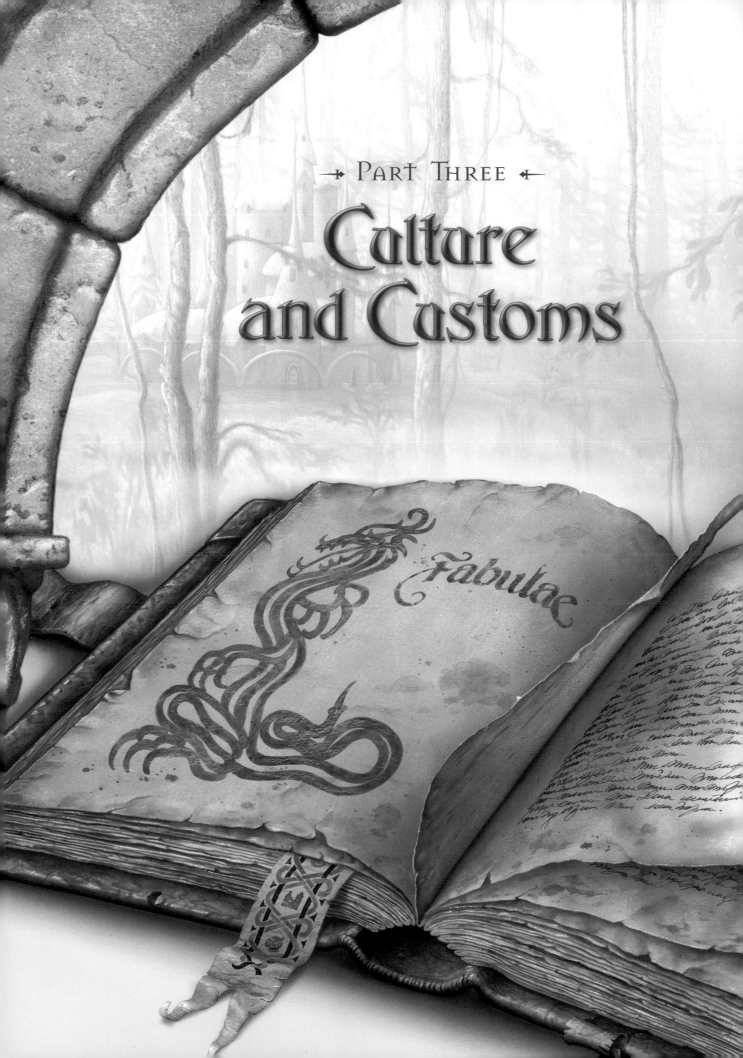

Part Three
Culture and Customs

Fabulae

Dragons and Magic

Dragons are well-versed in the art of magic, but not dreaded black magic. They work with so-called brown (or earth) magic, green (or plant) magic, and blue (or water) magic.

They know how and to what extent they can manipulate nature for their own purposes without disturbing the ecological balance for which they have always shown the utmost respect. They are able to invoke the power of the elements and can create illusions. They can invent disguises and maintain them for long periods of time, enabling them to escape their persecutors by appearing to be part of the landscape—or by masquerading as young children. There are countless legends in which human beings are transformed into monsters, evidence that originally these humans were young dragons who had not completely mastered their magic powers and were unable to maintain their illusory forms. Enormous powers of concentration are required to maintain a disguise for a long

time, and young dragons often lack the necessary skill. Adult males, however, are able to preserve their chosen disguises for many days at a time, although they do need rest at night. The great dragon wizards are able to maintain illusory forms for months on end with only brief rest periods.

These dragon wizards hate the clumsy human wizards, who, with no respect for the laws of nature, alter and often corrupt the life forces of the planet. The animosity is mutual. Human apprentices of magic envy the dragon's superiority in the occult sciences.

Indeed, the superior wisdom and tremendous power of dragons aroused the hatred of medieval necromancers and priests, who taught people that dragons were the incarnations of evil and the devil. In medieval bestiaries, the figure of a dragon represented depravity and the diabolical; thus, dragons were often represented as gargoyles.

74

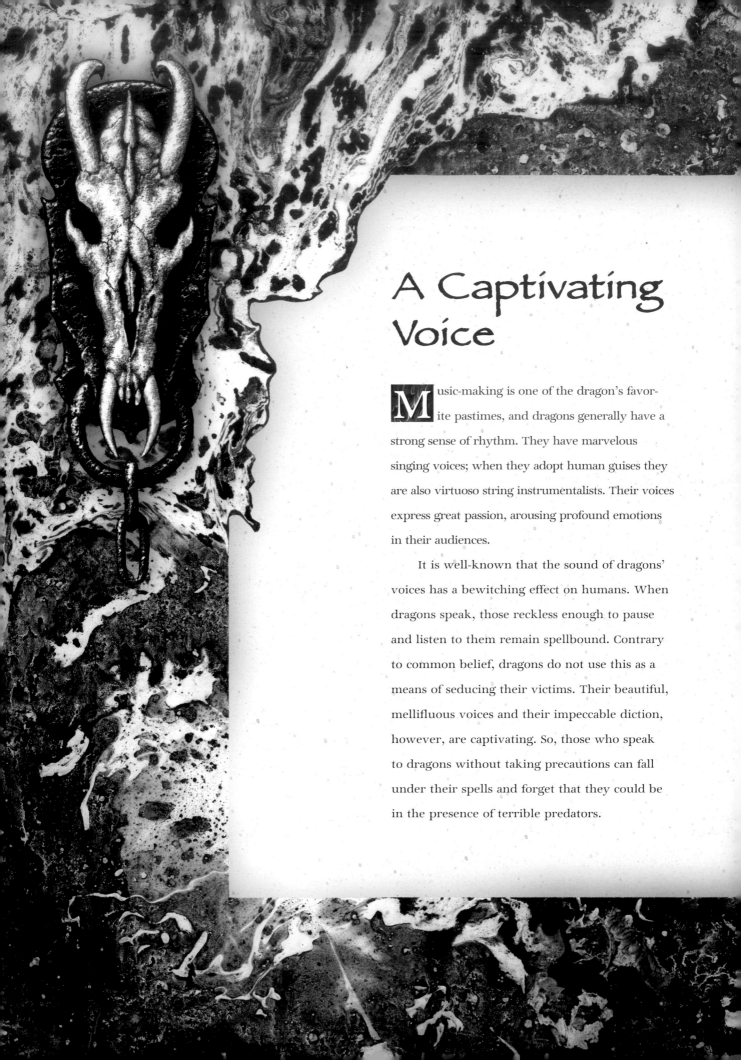

A Captivating Voice

Music-making is one of the dragon's favorite pastimes, and dragons generally have a strong sense of rhythm. They have marvelous singing voices; when they adopt human guises they are also virtuoso string instrumentalists. Their voices express great passion, arousing profound emotions in their audiences.

It is well-known that the sound of dragons' voices has a bewitching effect on humans. When dragons speak, those reckless enough to pause and listen to them remain spellbound. Contrary to common belief, dragons do not use this as a means of seducing their victims. Their beautiful, mellifluous voices and their impeccable diction, however, are captivating. So, those who speak to dragons without taking precautions can fall under their spells and forget that they could be in the presence of terrible predators.

Although talking to a dragon is highly
dangerous, a dragon does not usually go in for
surprise attacks or treachery, unless we are dealing
with a depraved creature dedicated to the cause
of evil.

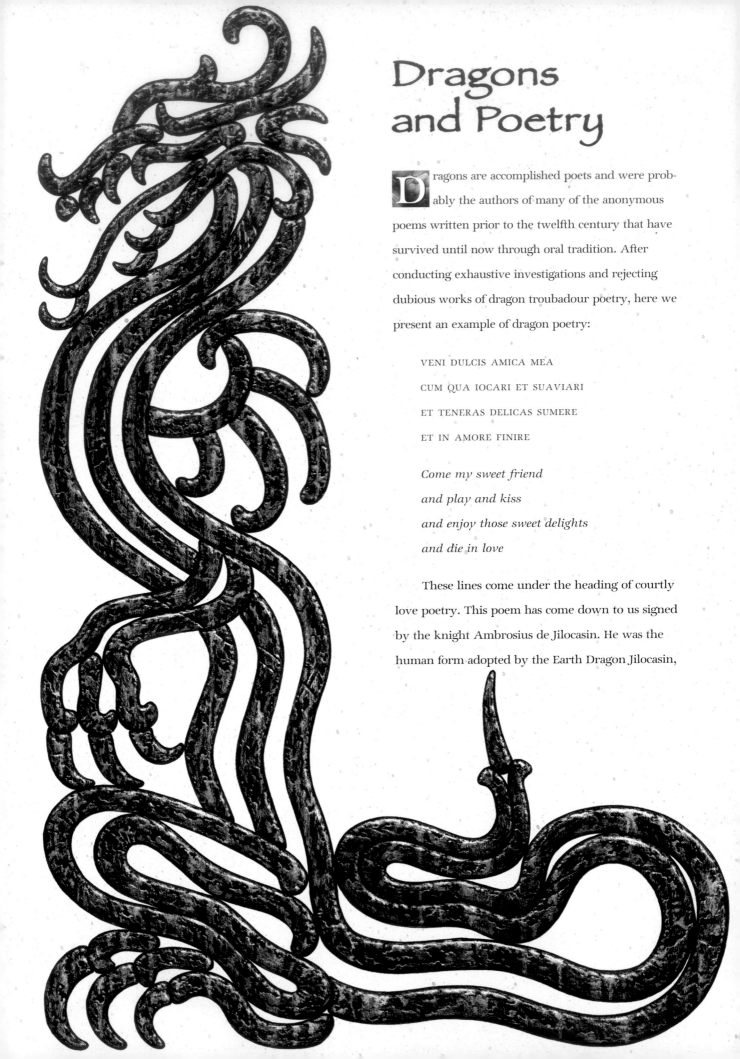

Dragons and Poetry

Dragons are accomplished poets and were probably the authors of many of the anonymous poems written prior to the twelfth century that have survived until now through oral tradition. After conducting exhaustive investigations and rejecting dubious works of dragon troubadour poetry, here we present an example of dragon poetry:

VENI DULCIS AMICA MEA

CUM QUA IOCARI ET SUAVIARI

ET TENERAS DELICAS SUMERE

ET IN AMORE FINIRE

Come my sweet friend
and play and kiss
and enjoy those sweet delights
and die in love

These lines come under the heading of courtly love poetry. This poem has come down to us signed by the knight Ambrosius de Jilocasin. He was the human form adopted by the Earth Dragon Jilocasin, the legendary father of two knights who distinguished themselves during the reign of Charlemagne.

Although we do not know who wrote the following poem, its subject is reminiscent of the story of the Dragon Prince and one of Eleanor of Aquitaine's ladies. The poem vividly evokes the heartbroken lover's tragic farewell. The unhappy Dragon Prince could well have parted from his lover with these very words:

DULCIS AMICA VALE, SINE TE
PROCUL HINC HABITATUS
ANXIUS ABSCEDO, QUI NON
CITO REDIAM
NON DISCEDO TAMEN TOTUS
RAMENETQUI TECUM
COGITAMEN MEUM. DISCEDO
VIX EGO MECUM.

Farewell sweet friend,
I must journey far from here without you
I depart in sorrow,
For I shall not return for many a year
But I shall not be gone completely
For my thoughts remain with you.
With heavy heart I take my leave.

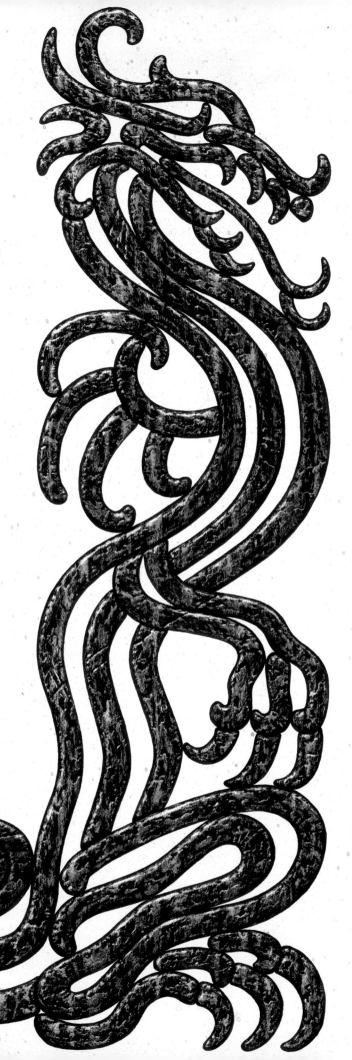

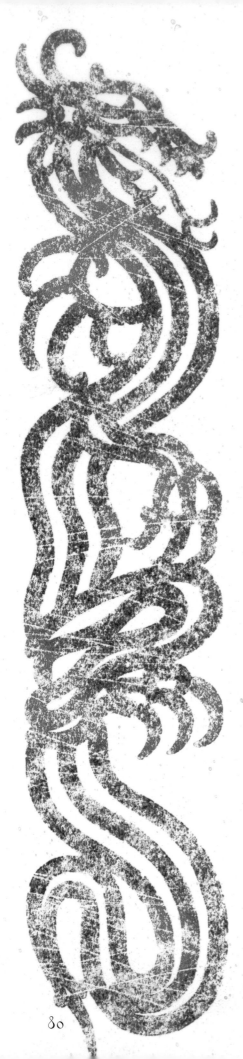

One of the most renowned poets, the mysterious Cercamon, was indisputably a dragon. For a while he was a very close friend of the famous Marcabrú, the brilliant troubadour from Gascony. Cercamon's style is musical and gentle, and was greatly influenced by this friend, as the following verse shows:

QUAN L'AURA DOUSSA S'AMARZIS
E L FUELHA CHAI DE SUL VERJAN
E L'AUZELH CHAJAN LOR LATIS,
ET IEU DE SAI SOSPIR E CHAN
D'AMOUR QUE·M TE LASSAT E PRES,
QU'IEU ANC NO L'AGUI EN PODER.

When the gentle breeze becomes embittered
and the trees lose their foliage
and the birds stop singing,
I too, sighing, sing of the love which
burns within me,
for it is not within my power to appease it.

There is also evidence of a lady troubadour of unknown origin who became famous for her happy verses and sweet songs. This was most unusual at a time when poetesses gave their verses to minstrels to sing, and her life remains shrouded in mystery.

She was called the Comtessa de Dia, and was, in fact, a young dragoness from the *Draco splendens* family. She was so bold and conceited that she did not stop at writing poems—four of which have come down to us intact—but she also became part of a band of wandering troubadours and even went so far as to make up her own life story.

AB JOI ET AB JOVEN M'APAIS

E JOIS E JOVENS M'APAIA,

CAR MOS AMICS ES LO PLUS GAIS

PER QU'IEU SUI COINDET'E GAIA;

E POIS EU LI SUI VERAIA

BE·IS TAING Q'EL ME SIA VERAIS,

C'ANC DE LUI AMAR NO M'ESTRAIS

NI AI COR QUE M'EN ESTRAIA.

He is young and happy

and I am young and happy,

my love is the most handsome

for him I am beautiful and elegant;

since I am true to him

he will always be true to me,

I will never betray his love

and I know my love will never betray me.

Dragons and Mankind

Throughout history, dragons and human beings have been unable to live peacefully side by side. As a result, mankind has not been able to benefit from ancient dragon knowledge. Man's craving for power and religious beliefs have kept Europe engulfed in interminable and bloody struggles. The Dragon Lords could not understand the reasons for man's self-destructive behavior and kept well out of the way, retreating to remote hiding places far from all this confusion.

Shrouded in mystery, dragons' trails remain lost in the obscurity of legend. But dragons do secretly pursue their quest for knowledge without completely excluding the human race, since they accept and teach those few men who seek the essence of truth.

Dragons and Ríddles

Dragons are very fond of conundrums and riddles, and often try to outsmart one another. The dragons most renowned for their mental prowess take part in competitions at the Council of the Dragon Father. Sometimes a free human being is admitted to these contests of wits, but only one single man has ever managed to beat his reptilian rivals in fair competition.

His name commands respect and admiration among both men and dragons, and upon him is

conferred the title of Lord of the Dragon. This man is Merlin the Magician, one of the few humans to win the affection of the dragon species. Due to his prudent use of his great magical powers and his innate respect for nature, Merlin also became the epitome of wisdom.

This is the riddle he solved to win the contest:

It is cold and it is hot
It is white and it is dark
It is stone and it is wax
Its true nature is of flesh
And its color is red

The answer is: THE HUMAN HEART.

Art and Jewels

Dragons are great lovers of art, especially of gold and silver work, and they love to hoard treasure. They are not renowned for their love of manual work, however, preferring intellectual activity by far. This is why they do not devote themselves to creating jewels, but to "acquiring" them from human beings through various methods: robbery, looting, trade, barter, fraud, or any other means fair or foul. It is interesting to note that the dragon code of honor does not consider it the slightest offense to steal from humans.

Dragons feel they can never have enough jewels, and they find it difficult to part voluntarily with one single treasure. For example, they give them to the favorites in their families, but they do so purely because they know the young maidens cannot

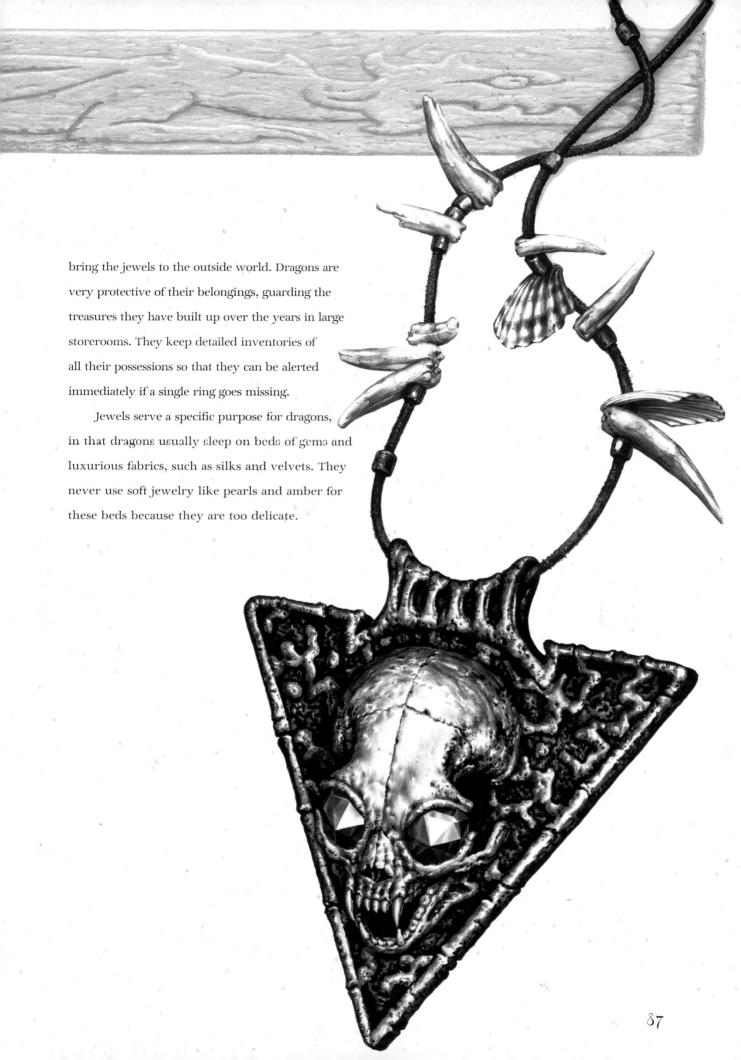

bring the jewels to the outside world. Dragons are very protective of their belongings, guarding the treasures they have built up over the years in large storerooms. They keep detailed inventories of all their possessions so that they can be alerted immediately if a single ring goes missing.

Jewels serve a specific purpose for dragons, in that dragons usually sleep on beds of gems and luxurious fabrics, such as silks and velvets. They never use soft jewelry like pearls and amber for these beds because they are too delicate.

The Dragons' Heritage

All dragons jealously guard very special ancient, shiny stones in their homes. Known as *Lapis draconiensis aurulucentis*, these stones have a natural phosphorescence. Dragons acquire them either as part of their inheritance or by looting, and they cannot be found just anywhere. These stones are sacred to dragons and they value them enormously, since they are a symbol of their identities.

There are a number of legends about these strange stones. Even though these stones are normally closely guarded, several hundred years ago gnomes stole some from a Norwegian dragon after it had been killed by a rival in a duel. Despite their great strength, no dragon has ever been able to retrieve them. Tradition has it that the stones come from a remote and wonderful place known as the Shining World, where the Ancestor Dragons still live.

In the distant past, some members of the dragon species were expelled from this world by the Great Dragon as a punishment for trying to change nature to suit themselves without respecting

ecological balance or life forces. They were allowed, however, to keep just a few shiny stones as a reminder of their homeland and their glorious past.

This explains the dragon's deep respect for nature and the care taken not to disturb ecological balance when practicing magic. Dragons believe that if they strictly observe dragon ethics throughout their lives, they will at last be able to return to the wondrous Shining World to join the Great Dragon, and be reunited with those who were not condemned to roam the Earth.

Due to this belief, most dragons do not abuse their strengths or power. Tragically, as dragons are intelligent beings with free will, there are some who stray from their code of ethics and take the path of darkness. These Servants of Evil engage in wars and battles with the sole aim of spreading grief and destruction.

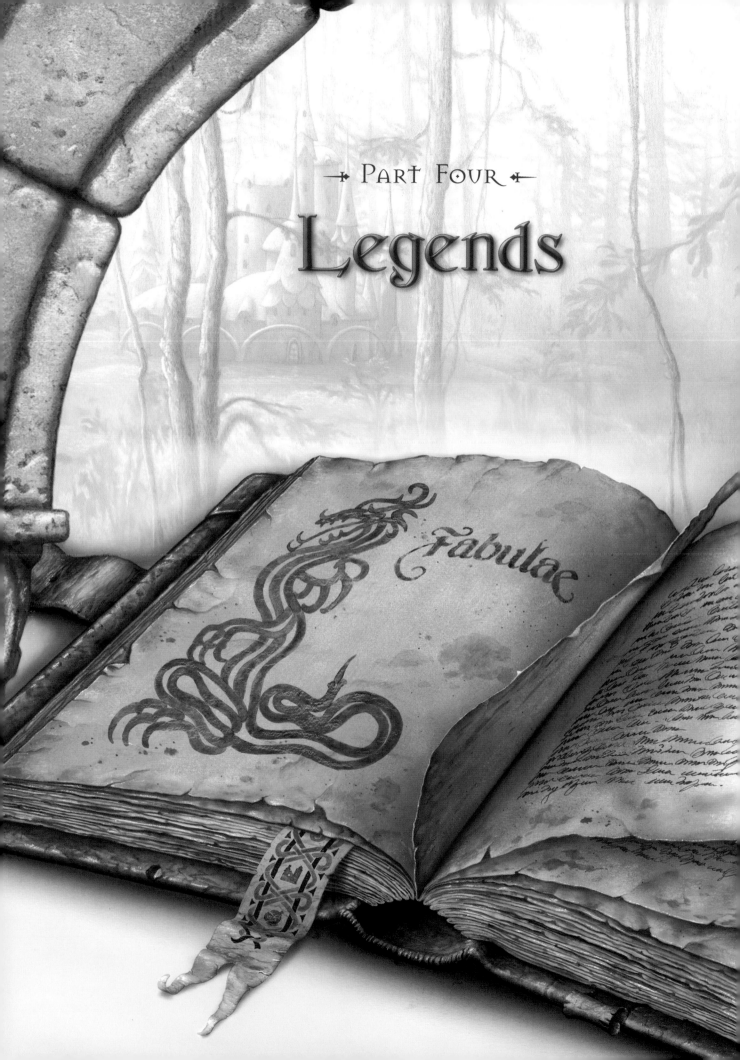

+ PART FOUR +

Legends

Fabulae

Perseus, Andromeda, and the Dragon

Long ago, Ethiopia was ruled by King Cepheus and Queen Cassiopeia, a vain woman who boasted that she was more beautiful than every one of the sea-nymph Nereids. Furious at this insult, the Daughters of the Sea complained to the god Poseidon, asking him to avenge them. He sent a dragon, who devastated the land and began devouring the young people of Ethiopia. The terrified population consulted the oracle Ammon, who told them that their only hope of deliverance was to hand over the beautiful Andromeda, daughter of the king and queen, to the dragon. Both monarchs were reluctant to surrender their daughter. Under pressure by their subjects, however, they finally agreed to the sacrifice.

The soldiers chained the maiden to a rock in the middle of the sea where the monster lived. Weeping and lamenting, the princess's parents waited on the shore.

It so happened that young Perseus, the son of Zeus, was passing that way on his winged horse Pegasus. On seeing the desperate sovereigns, the hero, who had just killed the terrible Medusa, stopped to ask them what was wrong. Sobbing, the king and queen told him their story.

"We are waiting for the dragon to come up and devour our daughter," they wailed. "If anybody can save her they will earn our gratitude, the hand of Andromeda, and the throne of Ethiopia."

Perseus found their offer most tempting, as the beauty of the maiden chained to the rock was evident, and the King was rich and prosperous. So Perseus donned a magic helmet of invisibility, which had been given to him by Hades, King of the Underworld, then he slipped his arm into a shining shield that had been a present from the goddess Athena—he was related to both these divinities. Brandishing a glittering diamond sword given to him by the god Hermes, Perseus rushed at the dragon.

Since the helmet made Perseus invisible, the monster was unable to defend himself. Andromeda naturally had no idea who was coming to her rescue. Perseus sliced through the dragon's flesh until he reached the heart, and gouged it out. Then he removed his magic helmet and revealed himself at last to the beautiful princess. With one stroke he cut through the chains that bound her to the rock, hoisted the maiden up onto his winged steed, and headed for the palace.

On reaching the royal palace, however, an unpleasant surprise was in store for him. Standing at the head of the army was Phineus, Andromeda's former suitor, claiming her as his wife. Perseus, reluctant to give up his well-deserved reward, took out Medusa's head from a linen bag and showed it to his enemies, who turned to stone at the sight.

Thus Perseus was able to marry the beautiful Andromeda unopposed. They had many beautiful children, one of whom fathered Alcmena, the mother of the powerful Hercules.

The Golden Apples

The most powerful of all the Greek heroes was Hercules, son of Jupiter and Alcmena. Eurystheus, King of Mycenae and Tiryns, was very jealous of Hercules, and sent him upon Twelve Labors. These labors included one almost impossible task: Hercules was to bring back the Golden Apples hidden in a divine garden guarded by the terrible dragon Ladon and the Daughters of the Night, who were known as the Hesperides.

The problem was that nobody knew where to find this garden.

Hercules obediently set out to find the mysterious place, for he was eager for great adventures. He searched, he questioned, and he inquired, but to no avail. Finally the sea-god Nereus directed Hercules to Prometheus, who told him what he wanted to know:

The Garden of the Hesperides lay in an enchanted place beyond the edge of the world, where Atlas, the father of the Hesperides, supported the vault of Heaven on his powerful shoulders.

The demigod set off immediately. He journeyed through unknown places full of danger, confronting monstrous and blood-thirsty creatures. At last, he arrived at the place where Atlas held up the sky on his shoulders. Nearby lay the beautiful garden surrounded by fragrant honeysuckle and rambling roses. The air echoed with the bubbling laughter of the beautiful nymphs, who were playing with the dragon, chasing each other through the trees.

Hercules, dressed only in a lion's pelt and wielding an enormous club, was afraid that his powerful weapon and aggressive appearance would frighten the Hesperides. Deciding not to enter the garden, he went over to Atlas and said, "Oh, powerful Atlas, you know the nymphs. Couldn't you go into the garden and pick the Golden

Apples? The nymphs won't be afraid of you. Meanwhile, I'll hold up the sky for you."

Atlas gladly agreed and hastily placed the celestial vault onto the shoulders of Hercules. Then, with a happy smile and a wave, he entered the garden.

From where he was standing, Hercules could hear shrieks of surprise and joy from the young women and the deeper voice of the dragon welcoming Atlas. For three days he heard nothing more of Atlas than the ringing of laughter from the fun and games in the divine garden. On the third day, Atlas appeared with the apples, which he placed at the hero's feet.

"Hercules, my friend," he said, "I have spoken with the very intelligent dragon, and he told me that the Hesperides are furious at losing the apples. Besides, I'm tired of holding up the sky without ever being able to have any fun. I tell you, I had a lovely time with Ladon and the nymphs. I'm leaving you here, my friend, to hold up the sky, and I'm going to live in the divine garden forever. But to show you that I have kept my word, I have brought you the apples. So don't hold it against me."

"That is good, I understand," Hercules assured him. "If I were you I would do exactly the same. But let me ask you just one favor."

"Ask me whatever you like," said Atlas.

"You may be able to hold up the celestial vault without effort, but I am not so accustomed to it and it's slipping. I'd like to put a rope cushion on my head to stop it from falling."

"That seems fair to me," replied Atlas. "I will hold it for you while you put the cushion on your head."

And the guileless Atlas held the sky so that Hercules could arrange the protective cushion on his head. The wily demigod, who was waiting for just that moment, ducked out of the way as fast as he could, picked up the apples, and fled.

"Dragon, dragon, he's escaping!" shouted the furious Atlas.

The dragon poked his head out of the garden gate and replied, "You are so stupid that you deserve your fate. I warned you not to trust Hercules. Now nobody can take your place."

So, as the Hesperides were calling him to play hide and seek, the dragon went back into the garden, leaving poor Atlas alone and bored with his burden.

Jason, Medea, and the Dragon

Jason was the son and legitimate heir of Aeson, the King of Iolcos. When the king died, however, the throne was usurped by Aeson's stepbrother, Pelias.

Fearing that Jason would try to seize the power that was rightfully his, Pelias decided to rid himself of his step-nephew in such a way that nobody would suspect him. He asked Jason to bring him the famous Golden Fleece, which was guarded by a terrible dragon who never slept.

The Golden Fleece was the skin of the magic winged ram sent by the god Hermes to rescue the brother and sister Phrixus and Helle from death. The ram carried them over the sea, but Helle fell into the water below, thereafter known as the Hellespont. Phrixus reached Colchis in Asia Minor. There he sacrificed the animal and gave it to Aeëtes, the king of that land, to thank him for his hospitality. The King of Colchis dedicated the Golden Fleece to the god Ares and hung it from a holm oak, guarded by the sleepless dragon.

Obeying his step-uncle's orders, Jason gathered together a group of brave men and set sail with them aboard a ship called the Argos. These brave men were called the Argonauts, after the ship. When Jason and the heroes of the Argos arrived at Colchis, they told the king that they had come to remove the Golden Fleece.

Though afraid of losing the precious treasure, King Aeëtes did not refuse to hand it over. Rather, he made a condition: Jason, unaided, would have to yoke two magic wild bulls that breathed fire from their nostrils and had bronze hooves. He would also have to sow the teeth of a defeated dragon. The dispirited hero did not think he could accomplish these tasks, but the king's daughter Medea was prepared to help him. The princess, who was a skillful sorceress, had fallen in love with the hero. She made Jason promise that if he succeeded in his tasks with her help, he would marry her and take her back to Iolcos with him. Jason found Medea beautiful and appealing, and agreed wholeheartedly.

Assisted by the clever princess, Jason yoked the bulls. When he sowed the dragon's teeth, a crop of armed warriors sprang from the ground and prepared to attack him. Following Medea's advice, Jason threw a stone in their midst and the warriors turned on one another. The triumphant hero went to King Aeëtes to demand the Golden Fleece.

"You've done well," said the king. "You have successfully carried out the difficult tasks I set for you. I rather suspect that you did not do this alone, but you are entitled to try to gain possession of

what you have come to seek. So go hence, try and take the Golden Fleece, which is hanging from a tree guarded by a dragon. This ferocious beast will not allow anybody to approach. Do not wound it or hurt it in the slightest, for it is a dragon dedicated to the god Ares. You must steal the Golden Fleece while the dragon is asleep. That is my last condition."

Waiting for the sleepless dragon to fall asleep seemed impossible, but Medea created a charm that lulled the dragon to sleep. Stealthily Jason and the Argonauts stole the Golden Fleece and fled to Iolcos aboard the Argos. Princess Medea fled with them, and together they went on to face new dangers.

Cadmus and the Dragon of Ares

genor, the King of Tyre and Sidon, had three sons and a very beautiful daughter named Europa. When Zeus, in the form of a bull, carried Europa off, the king ordered his sons to set off in search of her and not to return until she was found. The three young men set out, but soon realized the futility of their search.

One of the brothers, Cadmus, consulted the oracle at Delphi, and the oracle told him to abandon the search for Europa and found a city instead. To find the right place, he was instructed to follow a cow until the animal sank down from weariness.

Cadmus traveled on until he and the cow reached a lush, fertile valley, remote and unpopulated. The cow lay down to chew its cud near a river in a beautiful spot, and the young man decided that he would found his city in that very place. Seeing that the prophecy had been fulfilled, he sacrificed the animal to the goddess Athena. Then, overcome with exhaustion, he fell asleep.

A beautiful woman dressed in a white tunic appeared to Cadmus in his dreams. She was wearing a helmet and a gleaming breastplate. In her hands she held a silver lance and shield; on her shoulder perched an owl. Cadmus recognized her as Athena. The apparition spoke softly to him:

"Cadmus, brave warrior, you must indeed found your city here. To do so you must kill an enormous dragon that guards the spring dedicated to Ares, the god of war. Once you have vanquished it, pull out its teeth, plough a field, and scatter them."

The brave warrior prepared to fight the dragon that guarded the Spring of Ares. He fought a terrible battle against the beast. The powerful dragon used every possible trick, and Cadmus fought valiantly. The ground was soaked with blood, and rocks went flying as though they were pebbles. The yells of the hero and the roaring of the beast could be heard as far away as Mount Olympus. The terrible din of the contest disturbed the father of the gods, who was resting.

Annoyed, Zeus sent his daughter Athena to help Cadmus and put an end to this racket once and for all. Athena obediently appeared on the battlefield, but even with her help, it took Cadmus another day to defeat the powerful dragon. After killing the beast, the hero pulled out its teeth. He ploughed a field with great effort, scattered the teeth on the blood-stained and sweat-soaked soil, and waited.

Soon from the dragon's teeth sprang many fierce warriors who were called Sparti, or "Sown Men." They began to fight among themselves with uncommon determination until there were only five left. The hero then attacked and disarmed them.

The warriors acclaimed Cadmus as their king and lord, and helped him build the walls of the city of Thebes. Thanks to Athena's protection, the heroic Cadmus ruled thereafter in Thebes, a city famous for the courage of its warriors, for they had been born from the teeth of a dragon.

Sybaris of Cirfis

Legend has it that on the slopes of Mount Cirfis, close to the city of Delphi, an enormous female Water Dragon called Sybaris came to live. This beast terrorized the local population, for every month she demanded to devour a young, beautiful, and innocent adolescent boy, who had not yet tasted the sweetness of love. Apollo's priests selected the young men to be offered to the dragoness, drawing lots every month to see whose turn it was to be sacrificed.

It so happened that one day fate chose the young Alcyoneus, the most beautiful young man of that place, as Sybaris's victim. In addition to his valor and intelligence, Alcyoneus possessed a beauty that, like Ganymede's, entitled him to serve as cup-bearer to the gods.

The beautiful young man, crowned with roses and looking like a young Apollo, was led to the place of sacrifice amid a wailing and chanting crowd. Here the procession encountered Eurybatus, a brave young warrior. On seeing Alcyoneus dressed in a white tunic, the soldier detained the procession and asked, "Where did you find this boy, and where are you taking him?"

They replied, "Brave warrior, his destiny is tragic and his future is untimely Death, for he is the victim chosen by Destiny to be sacrificed to Sybaris."

Eurybatus turned pale with horror on discovering the boy's fate, and, following the impulse of his heart, asked them to free Alcyoneus.

"Sacrifice me in Alcyoneus's place," Eurybatus said, "for I have lived many years. This young boy has never tasted life. Let him enjoy the golden sun, fresh air, and the love he so deserves, for such a beautiful creature should be a favorite of Eros and Aphrodite and certainly not be overshadowed by the darkness of Hades."

The priests did not grant Eurybatus's petition, for they feared that the warrior, not being as young as the youth, would incur the dragoness's wrath against them. They did allow him, however, to join the procession.

On reaching the place designated by Sybaris for the sacrifice, they all withdrew except Alcyoneus and the warrior. The terrible dragoness came out of the cave thinking she would find a frightened and defenseless youth, but she met Eurybatus. The warrior launched a surprise attack on the beast and killed her. Thus the scourge of the dragoness in the area ended, and a sparkling spring appeared on the spot where the beast breathed her last gasp. Many years later, Eurybatus founded a city in Italy, which he called Sybaris in memory of this feat.

The Story of Melusine

This beautiful tale told by Jean d'Arras narrates the events that took place in the castle of Lusignan, in the French region of Poitou.

One day while out riding, the Lord of Lusignan met a beautiful woman, who told him her name was Melusine. Unaware of her true identity, the knight instantly fell passionately in love with the mysterious woman, and asked her to marry him. Eventually Melusine consented, on one condition: the knight could not look at her on Saturdays.

They lived happily for many years and had many children. Although Melusine seemed human, the children born of their union possessed some strange traits. They had rather nasty, huge teeth and unusually brilliant eyes. When the Lord of Lusignan, prompted by his jealous brother, broke his word and spied on his wife in her bath on a Saturday, he discovered to his horror that Melusine had changed into a dragoness.

The knight gave a howl of dismay, and Melusine discovered her husband's mistrust. She fled forever from the castle, and from that moment misfortune dogged the Lusignan heirs.

Local peasants say that each time a member of Melusine's family died, a dragon could be seen flying around the castle weeping copious tears. Tradition also has it that in the Poitou region a similar dragon was sighted flying over the area, weeping for the nobles who died during the French Revolution.

The Dragon Prince

In the High Middle Ages, the most renowned competitions of poetry in all of France were held at the court of Eleanor of Aquitaine. Once a year, celebrated troubadours gathered there to show off their art, and a winner of this poetic contest would be announced.

On one occasion, the winner was an unknown and handsome young man. He refused to give his name or say where he came from, despite the entreaties of Eleanor herself. There was an aura of mystery surrounding him. This, and his kindness and beauty, soon made him one of the favorites among the ladies of the court.

Griselda, a young and wistful maiden, the youngest daughter of the Lord of Foix, fell passionately in love with the stranger. Moved by the maiden's entreaties, the troubadour agreed to marry her in secret and take her to his home. He made one condition: Griselda should never try to see him other than when he chose, and she should never try to discover his identity. The lady, deeply in love, promised to comply with this strange condition. It seemed little to ask in exchange for being able to remain with her loved one.

One night, the young Griselda had fallen asleep in the arms of her beloved in Eleanor of Aquitaine's castle, where she lived. Suddenly, on opening her eyes, she found herself in an unfamiliar room. It was a luxurious place, adorned with silk and precious stones, and beside her lay her husband smiling benignly at her.

"You are in my mansion, which belongs to you," he said. "You may give orders to my servants and do whatever you please. There are stables with fine horses at your disposal, and huntsmen and hawks for hunting. You may come and go as you wish. You are my lady and wife, and all that is mine is yours. There are maidens ready to serve you and to carry out your every whim, dancers and musicians to entertain you, and jewels and silks to adorn you. If you need anything, tell me and I will give it to you."

"I only wish for your love, my lord," replied the young woman, bewildered.

"That is good, my love, but do not ever forget your promise."

Griselda demonstrated her compliance by flinging herself into the strong arms of her beloved husband. For a while this gentle lady kept her promise and believed she was in paradise. Her troubadour-knight husband, who was kind and passionate, spent most of his time with his wife. Occasionally, he would disappear into a locked room, but Griselda, faithful to her promise, did not ask him any questions.

Unfortunately, her curiosity gradually got the better of her, and one day she decided to find out the secret of her mysterious knight. She crept up to the door of the forbidden room, which he had left ajar, and spied through the opening. Aghast, she watched as her husband turned into a huge dragon with golden scales and powerful wings.

She could not prevent a cry of utter horror escaping from her lips. The Dragon Prince, thus revealed, wheeled around and saw his horrified wife in the doorway. Deeply hurt by her broken promise, the dragon bade his servants remove Griselda immediately to the court of Aquitaine, and never again did he return to see her.

The lady could never forget her beloved, and not a day went by without recalling the months of supreme happiness and bliss beside the disguised dragon.

Penitent and full of grief, she wrote down her adventure, which is how the famous story of the Dragon Prince found its way to us.

Jilocasin

During the reign of Charlemagne, there lived in the region of Gascony a very old and wise dragon called Jilocasin, who was a poet. Every so often, Jilocasin would abandon his comfortable, spacious dwelling and take on a human form to visit the king's court. There he was a well-known and respected troubadour, and would make the most of these brief sojourns to sing his verses and listen to the creations of other poets. Then he would return to his home in Gascony, where he could quietly compose and lead a peaceful life far from the world.

One day, he was traveling through the forests of Gascony, disguised as a troubadour, when he heard a desperate cry for help. Without losing a moment, he ran in the direction of the screams and came across a poor woman who was trying to defend herself against some bandits. Jilocasin changed back into a dragon and, with two mighty blows, finished off the ruffians. The woman had fainted from her injuries, so the dragon lifted her onto his back and flew her speedily back to his dwelling.

Jilocasin's servants took care of the lady, whose clothes, although they were torn and dirty, seemed to be those of a lady of high rank. While undoing the bundle that the lady was clasping to her breast, they found a baby boy only a few weeks old, slumbering peacefully, oblivious to everything.

Thanks to the care and solicitude of the servants, the lady soon came to, and Jilocasin took on his human shape to visit his protégée. The lady expressed her gratitude and told him her story.

She had been widowed within two years of marriage, and her family had forced her to marry her cousin, an unscrupulous man who was interested only in inheriting the title and wealth of her deceased husband. The wedding was celebrated in haste, before the mourning period prescribed by law had even been observed.

"I was pregnant by my first husband, but my cousin did not know," explained the lady, bitterly weeping. "When the baby was born, six months after the forced wedding, my husband tried to seize the baby to prevent him from claiming his inheritance. Desperate and fearing for the life of my son, I ran away. The villain pursued me with his henchmen, and he almost succeeded in killing my darling child. Fortunately, you saved us. Now my life belongs to you."

Touched by the grief and beauty of the woman, Jilocasin offered her support and shelter in his house. As time passed, the dragon-troubadour and the lady became inseparable. The beautiful fugitive, though aware of Jilocasin's true identity, was so taken by his kindness and amiability that it did not affect her love for him.

Meanwhile, Jilocasin found in her the understanding and friendship he had always sought. The dragon and the lady went for long walks together, and sometimes the dragon carried her on his back to visit far-off lands. Together, they rode, loved, and sang the verses that the dragon-poet composed.

They spent three happy years in this way. To complete their happiness, the lady became

pregnant. They were both looking forward to
the birth of their son, but she died tragically in
childbirth. Jilocasin was inconsolable. He had lost
an irreplaceable companion, the only woman who
loved him as he was.

Faithful to her memory, Jilocasin cared
for their two boys without making any distinction
between his adoptive son and his own son. He
taught them the highest ethical principals, in the
end presenting them at court to be armed knights.

The two brothers, who chose to be called
the Knights of the Dragon, were famous for
their nobility and honor. In the end, they
avenged their mother's memory by capturing
the castle that their villainous uncle had stolen
from them.

Tristan and the Fire Dragon

A long time ago, in the dark and heroic years of the Middle Ages, a terrible male Fire Dragon settled in the mists of Ireland, terrorizing the population on his nocturnal forays by burning everything he came across. In desperation, the King of Ireland publicly declared that he would give the hand of his daughter—the fair Isolde—to any knight who could deliver his country from the dragon.

At that time, there was a young knight at the Irish court called Tristan, a messenger sent by his uncle, King Mark of Cornwall, to ask for the hand of the beautiful Isolde for the king. The young man did not hold out much hope of accomplishing his mission, for the King of Cornwall was advanced in years, and he doubted that the beautiful princess would consider him a good match. On hearing the royal declaration, Tristan thought that if he could kill the dragon, the maiden would be his and he could take her to King Mark.

Knowing that water was dangerous for Fire Dragons, Tristan took a wine skin full of water and hung it over the door of the beast's lair. Then he lay in wait for the dragon to come out.

So fierce was the dragon, and so many deaths had he caused, that not even the most valiant knight in the kingdom dared challenge him. Hiding near the cave, watching to see what happened, was the majordomo of the royal household, who nursed a secret passion for Princess Isolde. The crafty old steward had no intention of killing the beast, for he was much too afraid. He was certain that by using his wits, however, he would be able to take advantage of the exploits of some brave knight and receive the credit for killing the dragon himself. From his hiding place, the astonished majordomo saw an unknown youth present himself before the creature's cave and call him in a loud voice.

When the dragon appeared, the wine skin full of water fell on him and quenched his fire. A fierce struggle ensued between the knight and the dragon. At last, after long hours of grueling combat, Tristan managed to kill the dragon, but he was so exhausted that he only had the strength to cut out and keep the dragon's tongue before losing consciousness.

At the sight of the slain dragon and the senseless knight lying on the ground, the treacherous steward decided to turn the situation to his advantage. With one stroke he cut off the dragon's head, and presented himself to the king as the author of the deed, claiming the promised reward. Isolde was in great despair, for she did not want the majordomo for a husband. She could not believe that the steward had succeeded in such a difficult task, so she paid a secret visit to the dragon's cave.

When she reached the cavern and saw the unconscious young man, Isolde understood that they had been tricked. She liked the knight's handsome features and, as she did not know of Tristan's plans, she sent her servants to bring the wounded man back to the palace in secret. There, she tenderly cared for him.

Two days later, the court gathered to announce officially that the dragon had been slain, and to give the triumphant majordomo the princess's hand. Proud as a peacock, the steward of the royal household stood at the foot of the throne waiting for his reward. Isolde, dressed in gold and silver, sat next to the king. The room was thronged with countless courtiers decked out in their finery. The king had not yet time to speak when Tristan burst into the room and asked for the hand of the princess.

"By what right do you ask for her?" asked the king, furiously.

"By the right of my sword and as the slayer of the dragon, your Majesty," replied the young man.

The entire court burst out laughing and the fury of the Irish monarch was very evident.

"You are presumptuous, young man. Perhaps you are unaware that the majordomo has killed the dragon?"

Then the beautiful princess broke in, for she could not help thinking that the unknown knight was much more handsome. She also realized his kisses would be much sweeter than those of the doddering steward. "Let him explain, Father, I implore you!"

"Very well," agreed the king. "Let the stranger speak."

"Let the dragon's tongue speak for me!" retorted Tristan.

"The dragon is dead, you impudent young man! How can he speak?"

"Look into his mouth, your Majesty!" exclaimed the hero.

The steward was thrown into confusion when they opened the beast's mouth and saw that its tongue was missing.

"Here is the missing tongue!" shouted Tristan, showing the astonished courtiers and the smiling Isolde the dragon's tongue that he had kept.

And so the majordomo's trick was discovered, and he was severely punished for his deceit. The king declared Tristan the winner. Tristan announced that he did not claim the princess's hand for himself, but for his uncle, Mark of Cornwall. The monarch was delighted at the news, for the King of Cornwall was rich. As for Isolde, she did not allow herself to be too disappointed by this announcement, for she had decided to win the heart of the valiant knight. The legend goes on to tell us how Tristan also fell in love with the beautiful princess. This love was to lead to a sad tale in which the two lovers ended up dying, unable to be parted.

The Peasant and the Dragon

One day, while flying back home, a male Earth Dragon was caught in a violent storm. The wind howled and the rain came down with such force that even the sturdiest oak trees were uprooted and blown around like pieces of straw.

Despite his great size, the dragon was buffeted in all directions by the darkening storm. In vain he tried and tried again to rise above the storm, battling with all his strength against the elements. At last, overcome with weariness, he fell to the ground, exhausted and lost.

While the dragon lay unconscious in the mud, a peasant named Lucas, who lived nearby in a humble shack, walked past. On catching sight of the creature, lying so still that he looked dead, Lucas was moved to pity for the poor dragon. He approached the inert body and, seeing that the dragon was still alive, he moved it, with the help of his horse, to an outbuilding that served as a barn. He made the dragon comfortable and covered him with a patched blanket, and ran into the house to ask his wife to prepare some hot food. She was apprehensive.

"You are mad if you want to give food and shelter to such a beast. You would do better to kill him, and then the king will give us a reward for his skin."

"Quiet, woman!" retorted Lucas. "The dragon is weak and ill, and it is not Christian to deny help to the ailing, whatever race they belong to."

"Don't be so stupid, husband!" exclaimed his

wife. "This creature is not a Christian, nor is he a man. He will eat you the minute he is better!"

Taking no notice of his wife's warning, the peasant devoted himself to feeding and caring for the beast. As a result of his efforts, the dragon soon recovered and thanked the peasant for saving him.

"There is nothing to thank me for; we are all God's creatures," replied the good man.

"Even so, many men in your position would have killed me and sold my skin, which is very valuable," said the thankful dragon.

"Any man who takes advantage of the fallen must be very evil. Such behavior does not befit a knight," replied the peasant.

On hearing her husband's words, the wife,

who was listening at the door, began to laugh. "Look at this fool, giving himself the airs of a knight when he is a pauper!" she exclaimed from her hiding place. "You won't speak like that when the tax collectors come and take away our horse because we haven't paid our taxes!"

"It is honor, not wealth, that makes a man a knight," replied the worthy Lucas in a low voice.

The dragon, however, heard the conversation. Noting the peasant's poverty, he offered him a reward for his trouble.

"I could not refuse anything in gold because the tax collector is coming soon and I have nothing to pay him with. But that is not why I helped you, my friend," said the man.

"I know, but now that I am strong enough to fly home, come to my cave and choose anything you wish."

Lucas climbed fearlessly onto the dragon's back, while his wife begged him not to trust the dragon.

"When you are in the middle of the forest, he will eat you," she groaned. "I will be left all alone!"

The dragon bore the peasant to his cavern, and there he entertained him for three days. When the time came for him to return home, the beast loaded a huge sack of gold and precious stones onto his back as a gift. He then carried Lucas back to his humble shack.

"Come and see me whenever you are needy," the dragon said on parting.

On arriving home, Lucas found his wife sad and dressed in mourning, for she believed her hus-band was dead. The woman was ecstatic when she saw him and his treasure. With the dragon's gifts, the couple were able to buy a beautiful farm with many animals. The wife, however, started becoming extravagant, and one day she said to her husband:

"If we had a little more money, we would be able to buy good land and employ others to work on it. Then, when we have a son, he would be able to be a knight. Why don't you ask the dragon for a little more gold?"

Lucas at first refused, but in the end he gave in and went to see the dragon. The creature thought it was a sound idea and was delighted to be able to help his friend once more. But hardly a year went by before his wife begged again, "If we could buy a castle and some villages, we would become counts."

Lucas, tired of his wife's nagging, went once more to see the dragon in his cave, and once more

was his request granted. The couple received a dukedom. Not long afterwards, the wife, with newfound airs and graces, wanted to go and live at court.

One day the wife, now having been made a duchess, saw the Queen arriving in her golden carriage, dressed in silks, with silver farthingales, and wearing fabulous jewels.

Her eyes glinting with ambition, the wife said, "My good Lucas, it has occurred to me that when we have a son, if there is a war he will have to go to the front as an officer, perhaps dying in combat. It would be much better if we became monarchs so our son would be safer. Your friend the dragon would grant us this wish."

"But wife, don't talk nonsense!"

His wife, however, cried and entreated him until finally Lucas agreed to visit the dragon again.

"My friend," said the dragon warmly, after listening to his story, "your wife is too ambitious. She will never leave you in peace. She will never have enough and she will always want more—but I have the answer. Come into the cave."

The dragon showed his guest into a cozy room where beautiful young women were singing and dancing.

"Now you are my prisoner. These girls will keep you company and will see that your every wish is carried out, and you will not return to see your wife."

From then on the good man lived happily with the dragon and the maidens. As for Lucas's wife, she had to dress in mourning once more, convinced that her husband had finally been devoured by the dragon, just as she had predicted from the beginning.

The Tarasque

There is an ancient legend that explains how, in the High Middle Ages, there lived a huge male Water Dragon at the bottom of a deep lake in the south of France. He was known as the Tarasque and was covered in splendid steely-blue scales.

The local population was terrorized by the presence of the beast, who would emerge from the lake from time to time and devour a virgin, as is customary among Water Dragons.

The villagers did not know what to do to free themselves from the Tarasque. Nobody was brave enough to fight him, nor was there anybody who would even dare to speak to him to negotiate a truce. In the end, the people decided to send emissaries to the King of France's court. The king, however, had other serious problems to deal with and was not interested in the troubles of a village so far from the capital. Nor were the knights of the court interested in the problem. The dragon did not guard any treasure that would make the challenge worth their while, nor was he holding a princess prisoner whom they could free to gain honor and glory.

"The dragon only devours humble, ignorant, and filthy peasants. The tournaments and jousts are much more profitable," thought the greedy knights.

In desperation, the local people gathered to discuss the possibility of abandoning the village, given that they were unable to rid themselves of the dragon. The arguments were becoming heated, when Saint Martha—who was known and worshipped in the region for her goodness and bounty—appeared to them in an apparition.

The village elders, interpreting her appearance as a sign from the heavens, went to meet her to ask for help and beseeched her desperately. In response to the villagers' urgent entreaties, the saint offered to capture the Tarasque, on one condition.

"Tell us what you require, good saint," said the local people.

"I just want you to pray to God for three days, asking Him to help me overcome the Tarasque," replied Saint Martha.

The elders accepted her condition and waited, full of faith that a miracle would happen to save them forever from the curse.

So, one morning, the saint made her way to the lake where the Tarasque lived. Despite his ferocity, the dragon was a great music lover.

The beautiful Saint Martha stood on the shore and began singing praises to God and to the Virgin Mary in a beautiful, passionate voice. Enchanted by the sweetness of her songs, the Tarasque came out of the water and lay down at her feet. The saint quickly tied her eglantine belt around the dragon's neck without the beast offering the slightest resistance.

The dragon was completely subdued. Saint Martha led him easily to the village, where he was killed by the peasants.

In memory of this feat, the region where the Tarasque lived was known thereafter as Tarascon.

La Vibria

The history books tell us that many years ago a certain Count Jofre el Pilós governed most of the Catalonian territories. There lived a monstrous dragoness in a cave in the Massif of Sant Llorenç. She was known by the chilling name of La Vibria.

When the dragoness was still young, she was placed in the cave by the Moors, who wanted to avenge themselves on the Christians who had expelled them from the region. The creature grew into a most powerful beast. During her nocturnal forays into the surrounding countryside, she devoured sheep and shepherds, devastating farms and terrorizing the distraught local people.

The mayor of Terrassa offered a substantial reward to whoever could free the town from this terrible menace. Many knights, monks, and soldiers tried to kill La Vibria, but as she was an exceedingly cunning dragoness, well-versed in magic, no one could subjugate her.

Finally, Count Jofre, tired of the creature's excesses and of his subjects' sorrows, decided to confront her. Fully armed, and riding his powerful black steed, the count set out for the dragoness's cavern. The place was deserted, and a solitary black raven—the dragoness in disguise—was perched on a branch. The brave Jofre, however, was not taken in by La Vibria's trick, and he shouted her secret name: "Vibria!"

The dragoness immediately abandoned her bird disguise and turned into the repulsive winged beast that she really was. Then she seized the count with her sharp talons, and tried to lift him off the ground and crush him against the rocks. Without flinching, Count Jofre lashed out bravely against the beast's scaly neck. When she opened her enormous slimy jaws, he plunged his sharp sword down her soft gullet, wounding her fatally.

The dragoness managed to fly off, but she fell headlong into the mountainside. This summit has been known ever since by the name of Puig de la Creu—the "Peak of the Cross."

In time, Count Jofre founded a convent of nuns near the cave. He also had a monastery built on the top of the mountain, so that never again would a dragon make its home among the rocks where La Vibria had lived.

Count Jofre's battle against La Vibria is, in fact, recorded for posterity above the ancient sculpted Gate of Sant Iu, in a transept of Barcelona Cathedral, where it can still be seen today.

The Dragon of Mont Blanc

The peaceful little village of Mont Blanc was a very happy place. It was governed by a good, wise king, and had a healthy economy. The king had a beautiful daughter who was loved and respected by everyone. The only cloud on the horizon was that the villagers were not sufficiently pious and they often forgot to offer up gifts to the gods, which considerably angered the pagan priests.

Legend has it that one beautiful midsummer's day an enormous male Water Dragon with brilliant green-blue scales rose out of the river. The horrendous beast appeared before the terrorized people and spoke to them.

"Every month you must bring me a beautiful young virgin for my food," he crooned in a sing-song voice. "Otherwise, I will destroy your homes and your fields, your crops and all your livestock. If you obey me, I promise I will not attack anybody, and I will allow you to live in peace."

The horrified villagers ran to the palace to tell the king of their misfortune.

Much to his sorrow, the king had to accept the dragon's conditions. In vain, the people entreated the gods to liberate them from the terrible beast; in vain, the priests of the pagan cults offered up sacrifices and gifts to the gods to rid them of the curse.

Several months went by, and at every new moon a young virgin girl was handed over to the hungry dragon. The situation became absolutely unbearable. In the homes where they were not weeping over a sacrificed daughter, they feared for the fate of their children. Soon, there were almost no virgins left.

The month of April came, almost a year since the arrival of the beast, and with the scarcity of virgins, the dragon's next victim happened to be the king's own daughter. She had insisted on taking part in the lottery of young girls destined to be sacrificed.

Resigned to her fate, the girl spent the night in Christian prayer. In the morning, she attired herself in a white tunic tied with a sweetbriar belt. Then, crowned with flowers, she bade farewell to her grief-stricken parents and the weeping villagers. With a strength of mind inspired by her faith, the girl made her way alone to the dragon's cave. Here, the beautiful girl calmly awaited her end, praying all the while.

The legend describes how the people gathered all along the walls of the village, weeping and wailing, awaiting the beast to come out of his cave. Everyone stood silently to witness the imminent tragedy.

Suddenly an unknown knight arrived, galloping speedily on a white charger with a glittering mane. His weapons shone like silver and his cloak was as red as glowing embers. His shield was emblazoned with a red cross on a burnished gold background.

Without dismounting or reining in his horse, the stranger charged at the beast. Overwhelmed by the power of the magnificent horseman, the dragon retreated and tamely lay down.

"My lady," said the stranger, "tie the eglantine belt from your tunic around the dragon's neck and he will follow us meekly." The girl fearlessly carried out his instructions, and the dragon allowed himself to be led away without offering any resistance. The strange procession made its way to the gates of the castle, where the inhabitants of the village were waiting in utter astonishment.

The girl ran to embrace her parents, the king and queen, while the pagan priests boasted that they had defeated the creature with their offerings and rituals. The knight asked for silence, and the whole assemblage listened to the words of their mysterious and valiant savior.

"I am George, the soldier of Christ," he said. "I am devoted to Him. This young Christian girl prayed for help, and that is why I was given the mission of saving her from Death. May the Cross which has saved you crown this village forever after. Abandon your false idols and you need never fear the dragon again." And to confirm his words, the young knight traced the sign of the Cross above the docile beast.

Immediately, the dragon was transformed into a rosebush with roses as red as blood. Still today, in several European countries, the name of Saint George is associated with red roses as a reminder of the knight who rid them of the terrible dragon forever.

Tannin and the Prophet Daniel

Many, many years ago, several centuries before the birth of Christ, in sumptuous and pagan Babylon, there lived a young exile from Jerusalem, who was to become a famous prophet. The king of the Babylonians, Cyrus the Persian, held the young man, Daniel, in high esteem because of his wisdom, often inviting him to his table for consultation.

The prophet, however, who came from the tribe of Judah, was not able to convince the powerful monarch that the stone and metal idols that the Babylonians worshipped were false.

At that time, in the city of Babylon, there lived a male dragon named Tannin, who was worshipped as a god. Tannin had made a pact of friendship and goodwill with the Babylonians and lived in the Temple of Bel. There, in the precincts, priests and servants took care of Tannin's every need, and Cyrus often visited him. Tannin was an ancient and extraordinarily wise purple dragon with such an uncommon beauty that he was considered divine.

One day, when Daniel had proved the falsity of the god Bel to the Babylonian monarch, Cyrus asked him angrily, "Why don't you worship Tannin as a god? You cannot deny that the dragon is alive; he is not made of stone or metal like the other gods in this land."

"He is alive but he is not a god, for he can die and gods do not die," replied the prophet.

Cyrus retorted, "He has been alive since the time when my father was young, and even long before that. He has lived in the temple for countless generations of men, and there is nobody alive who can remember when he was born. Our beloved Tannin speaks with utmost wisdom, and he is very knowledgeable. I do not believe that he will ever die. He is, without doubt, a god."

Daniel then wanted to show the king that the dragon could die and was therefore no different from other creatures. He made cakes of pitch, sheep's fat, and wool, giving them to the unsuspecting Tannin.

The dragon, accustomed to being given food by men, did not realize the trick and ate them. The poisoned cakes soon began to work, and the poor dragon died in agony within two days. And so Cyrus, King of the Babylonians, was convinced that Tannin was mortal, and he lost his wise dragon-god forever.

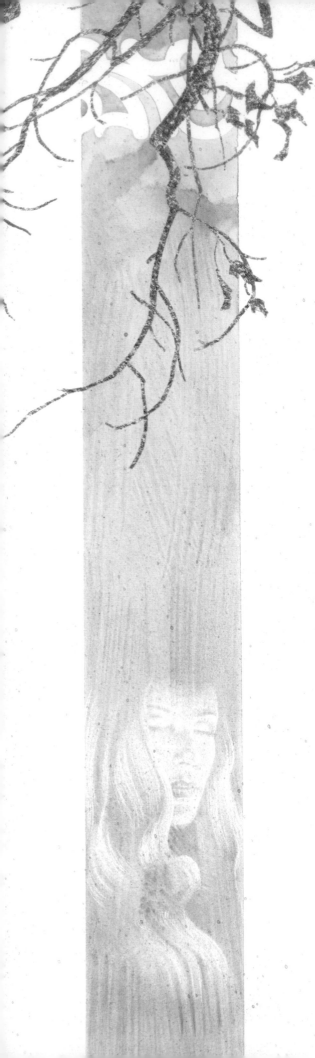

The Cuelebre

In a hut in an Asturian village in Spain lived a very beautiful maiden, who was vain and forever daydreaming. She spent hours and hours combing her long flowing hair by a spring. There was nothing she loved more than to admire her beautiful reflection in the limpid green water of the pool. In vain her mother and grandmother warned her, "It is dangerous to comb your hair by the spring. Be careful, because if one single hair falls and ruffles the surface of the water, the spirit of the spring will bewitch you."

"Old wives' tales!" cried the girl. "There is no spirit in the fountain."

The girl, however, was very wrong. In this pool there lived a powerful spirit, one of those nymphs of the streams and mountains that abound in Asturian mythology. The spirit watched angrily as the girl spent the whole day combing her hair, never helping to spin the wool or knead the dough. She had not been able to do a thing about it, as the girl did not ruffle the water of the pool, but patiently the nymph waited and waited for her chance.

Then, one day, one of the girl's golden hairs fell into the water. The nymph, dressed in a magic cloak of green water, rose angrily out of the pool.

"Didn't your mother warn you not to ruffle the water?" she asked in a very quiet voice.

"A hair as beautiful as mine cannot ruffle water," replied the proud maiden.

"I am going to bewitch you to punish you for your pride!" the spirit exclaimed icily. With her long golden hair adorned with pearls and a crown made from moonbeams, the nymph stepped out of the dark pool. Frowning, the nymph declared, "I am turning you into a Cuelebre dragon. You will only turn back into a maiden if you meet a knight who is so brave that he is not afraid of you and has a heart so pure that he is able to perceive the beauty hidden within your soul."

At once the girl's body grew to an enormous size and became covered with colored scales. Her golden hair turned into glittering crests, and two wings sprouted from her shoulders. With a howl of despair, the Cuelebre dragon slunk off weeping inconsolably, and hid in a dank cave by the sea. Now, as all the youths who have set eyes on the poor creature have been afraid of her appearance, the proud girl who was bewitched by the spirit of the spring still lives in her little cave on the seashore. Here she waits and longs for the knight who will see her hidden beauty, so that she can become a maiden once again.

Siegfried and Fafnir

Odin, the father of the Norse gods, told the giants to build a beautiful castle called Valhalla. The builders demanded in return Freyja, the goddess of beauty.

When the castle was finished, the gods wanted to rescue Freyja from the giants, but the giants demanded a suitable ransom: the Rhine gold treasure which the Nibelung dwarves had hoarded. So the gods were forced to steal the dwarves' treasure and hand it over to the giants. Fafnir, one of the giants, kept all the gold for himself and transformed himself into a dragon to guard the treasure in a cave.

Mime, though being a strong dwarf, was desperate, for the dwarves could do nothing against the dragon. When he learned that Sigmund, hero of the Volsung, had died in battle, he decided to take charge of the now fatherless little Siegfried and turn him into a warrior as brave and strong as the deceased hero.

The dwarf became his tutor, with the intention of getting him to steal the treasure guarded by the dragon. When Siegfried came of age at eighteen, Mime gave him the broken fragments of his father's sword, the magic Gram, teaching him how to forge the sword anew. When the sword was whole again, Mime told Siegfried about the dragon Fafnir, but not about the treasure.

"What a great adventure it would be, young Siegfried, if someone as strong and brave as you succeeded in killing the dragon!" said Mime, to entice him. The bold Siegfried agreed to undertake the task and lost no time in making his way to the dragon's cavern.

On arriving at the beast's lair, he called him loudly. Fafnir awoke and came out, intending to devour the thoughtless intruder. Fearlessly, the hero brandished the magic Gram and withstood the dragon's attack. When Fafnir reared his ghastly head, Siegfried plunged the sword into the beast's neck.

Mortally wounded in the jugular, the beast collapsed in a pool of blood. A few drops of blood splashed on Siegfried's lips, giving him the miraculous faculty of understanding the language of the birds. Some sang, "Here's young Siegfried, who has just killed the dragon. If he were to bathe in the monster's blood, he would become invincible."

Others chimed, "He is not as clever as he seems, if he doesn't realize that Mime will betray him. The dwarf only wanted the treasure that Fafnir was guarding, and now that the dragon is dead, he will kill Siegfried."

The young man followed the birds' advice and bathed himself in the dragon's blood. From then on, he became totally invulnerable.

A lime leaf fell on his shoulder, however, while he was bathing, and this tiny little patch of his body was not protected by the magic blood. This was later to be his undoing.

Later on Siegfried killed the artful Mime, who only wanted the treasure. And so our hero went into the dragon's cave wielding Gram, the famous magic sword. Siegfried—still being advised by the birds—salvaged a magic helmet of invisibility and the dwarf's ring, which were among the wonderful precious objects in the cave.

After this, he sheathed the powerful Gram and set off in search of new adventures.

The Gypsy and the Dragon

In the vast steppes of Russia there lived a tribe of gypsies, who traveled up and down the country selling herbal remedies and beads, never staying for long in the same place. The leader was an astute and sharp-witted man named Yuri, who had six clever sons. One day, when the tribe was camped next to a town celebrating the Feast of Saint Basil, Yuri was told that a farmer who lived a few leagues from there was selling colts at a very good price.

The astute Yuri thought that he would broker a good deal if he bought the animals and then sold them again. Putting a piece of fresh cheese and a slice of rye bread in a pouch, and leaving his gypsy folk to sell their wares at the fair, Yuri set out cheerfully on his way to the farmer's village.

On arriving in the village, he was surprised to find the place silent and deserted. He walked through the muddy, narrow streets in astonishment, looking for clues as to what had happened. Suddenly, he heard a terrified voice warning him:

"Flee from here, you stupid man, if you don't want the dragon to devour you!"

"Who is speaking?" asked Yuri.

"It is I, old Vestia."

Then, from behind some filthy willow baskets, emerged an old man with a long white beard. He was stooped and trembling and so thin that he was nothing more than skin and bone.

"Hello, granddad!" said Yuri amiably. "What's going on here?"

"Oh my son!" sighed the old man. "An evil dragon has devoured all the inhabitants of the village—people and animals, even the cats! I am the only person left because I am so old that the dragon doesn't fancy eating skin and bones. Today he is due to return, and as he will find nothing else to eat, he will eat me! Go far away from here if you don't want to suffer the same fate!"

"Don't worry, granddad," replied the bold Yuri. "I am not afraid of the dragon. If you do what I tell you, no harm will befall you. Hide among the willow baskets and don't say a word."

Soon the earth began to shake and tremble from the dragon's steps. He was enormous and looked very hungry.

Yuri, who knew that dragons are vain and curious by nature, went up to him and greeted him courteously: "Good day, Tsar of the Dragons!"

The dragon was very proud to be addressed so regally. Showing off, he thrashed the ground with his tail, spreading his wings to display the marvelously jeweled breastplate adorning his chest. Then, bowing his head, he said modestly, "But that is not so. I am simply a common dragon."

"You are not common, magnificent lord," protested Yuri. "You are the greatest, the most beautiful, and the most powerful of all! I am eager for you to show me your strength."

"Yes," admitted the vain creature, coiling and uncoiling his tail and blushing with pleasure, "it's true I am strong and I am generally thought to be beautiful. But who are you, standing before me so fearlessly?"

"I am the strongest man in the world," replied Yuri tauntingly.

"You are the strongest? Don't make me laugh!"

"But I really am, even though you doubt my words," responded Yuri.

The dragon, who by now was very interested in the bold gypsy, picked up a stone and crushed it to powder.

"Perhaps you can do the same, if you are the strongest of humans!"

"That wouldn't be difficult," replied Yuri with aplomb. "Can you squeeze water out of a stone as I can?" Then, without letting the dragon see what he took from his pouch, he squeezed the fresh cheese until the whey trickled out between his fingers.

"Well," thought the dragon, "he really is very strong. It would be better to have him as a friend than an enemy."

To win the man's friendship, he suggested, "Come and eat at my house. You are a very nice human being and I would like us to be friends."

"Very well, Mr. Dragon, let's go!"

The beast took Yuri to the cave where he lived and asked him, "Would you kindly go to the woods and bring back an oak tree to make a fire?"

Yuri went out determined to prevent the dragon from discovering a planned trick, as his arms were not strong enough to uproot such enormous trees and bring them back to the cave. So he got the idea to tie a group of sturdy oaks together with the rope the dragon had given him.

After a while, seeing that the gypsy had not returned, the beast made his way to the woods. There he met Yuri, who was very busy tying the trunks carefully together.

"What on earth are you doing?" asked the dragon, astonished.

"Well, I thought that if I bring back all the trees at once, we will have wood for several days."

"Leave it! Leave it! We don't want to cut down the whole wood!" exclaimed the dragon, more and more convinced of his friend's strength. "I will take the trunk back home. While I'm gone, bring me home a bullock to cook. Behind the house, in a field, you will find a fine herd of bullocks. Just make sure you choose the plumpest."

Yuri set off determinedly for the field. After a while, the dragon found him tying the bullocks together.

"What are you doing?" asked the dragon.

"Well, I thought if I brought all the bullocks back to the cave we could make a huge delicious bullock stew."

"My dear friend," said the dragon, sighing, "you have a very strange way of doing things. One bullock will be quite enough. I'll take it home myself." Then, somewhat perturbed by his guest's behavior, the dragon seized and killed the plumpest bullock, then skinned it and started to cook it. The two friends gorged themselves until they were

fit to burst. After the sumptuous feast, the dragon, who was in a good mood, offered to accompany the gypsy back to his home.

"Thank you," replied Yuri, "but I was thinking of buying some horses."

"Don't worry about that—I have a beautiful colt, and I can sell it to you for a hundred rubles."

Yuri agreed to the deal and told the dragon that he would pay him once they had reached his home at the gypsy camp. As it was a long way, the dragon decided to adopt a human form. They set out on horses belonging to the dragon, and made good progress toward the camp. During the journey, Yuri warned his friend that he had six sons who were strong and had clairvoyant powers. When they reached the outskirts of the camp, Yuri's sons ran to meet him. Seeing the colt, they all began to shout:

"You've only brought one!"

"It must be for me," shouted the oldest.

"No, no, I want this one with the enormous eyes!" argued the smallest.

Yuri looked at the dragon and said, "What rascals! Didn't I tell you that they were clairvoyant? They have recognized you!"

The poor terrified dragon thought that the boys wanted to keep him as a plaything.

He even thought they might have wanted to devour him. He also thought they could be as strong as their father and there would be no possibility of escape. So he quickly dismounted from his horse and took on his dragon form, flying off in panic. Never again did he dare go near the Russian steppes, for he had come to believe that gypsies were so strong, they would fight to capture dragons.

Epilogue

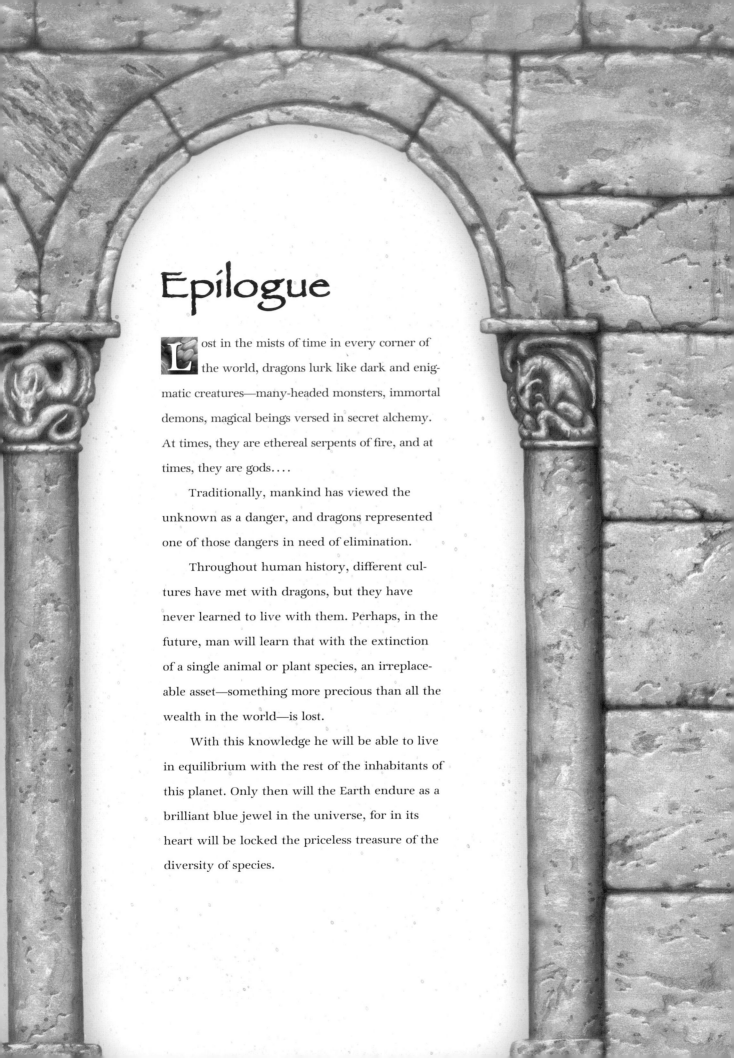

Lost in the mists of time in every corner of the world, dragons lurk like dark and enigmatic creatures—many-headed monsters, immortal demons, magical beings versed in secret alchemy. At times, they are ethereal serpents of fire, and at times, they are gods....

Traditionally, mankind has viewed the unknown as a danger, and dragons represented one of those dangers in need of elimination.

Throughout human history, different cultures have met with dragons, but they have never learned to live with them. Perhaps, in the future, man will learn that with the extinction of a single animal or plant species, an irreplaceable asset—something more precious than all the wealth in the world—is lost.

With this knowledge he will be able to live in equilibrium with the rest of the inhabitants of this planet. Only then will the Earth endure as a brilliant blue jewel in the universe, for in its heart will be locked the priceless treasure of the diversity of species.

Index

Abodes, 30, 45
　of Earth Dragons, 46–48
　of Fire Dragons, 66
　of Water Dragons, 60
Acute gastritis *non virginae*, 23
Aeëtes, King, 96–97
Alcyoneus, 100–102
Ameisenhaufen, Professor Peter, 67
Ancestor Dragons, 88
Andromeda, 92
Apollo, 100
Ares, 96, 97, 98
Athena, 92, 98
Atlas, 94–95

Black magic, 26, 74
Book of the Golden Dragon, 68
Breastplates, jeweled, 27, 45

Cadmus, 98
Caves and caverns, 30, 46, 48, 60, 62, 66
Celestial Dragons, 68
Cercamon, 80
Colonies, 62, 66
Coloring, 27, 29
　of Earth Dragons, 40
　of eggs, 34, 43
　of Fire Dragons, 62, 66, 67
　of the Golden Dragon, 68
　of Water Dragons, 50, 58
Comtessa de Dia, 80
Council of the Dragon Father, 32, 35, 45, 49, 84
Cuelebre, The, 130–131

Da Silva, 56
Daniel, 128–129
*Diary of Expeditions and Discoveries of the
　New World*, 56
Disguises and illusory forms, 35, 74, 76
Draco flameus (See "Fire Dragons")
Draco flamula (See "Little Fire Dragons")
Dragon of Ares, 98
Draco rex Cristatus (See "The Great Earth Dragon")
Draco splendens (See "Water Dragons")
Dragon Father, 21, 32, 35
　in Earth Dragon society, 49
　in Fire Dragon society, 62, 66
　　(*See also* "Council of the Dragon Father")
Dragon of Mont Blanc, The, 51, 125–127
Dragon Prince, The, 79, 106

Dragonesses, 32, 34–35, 36, 66, 80
　and mating, 35, 42–43, 56
　in legends, 100–102, 104, 122–124
Dragons' ladies, 37, 60

Earth Dragons, 40–49
　abodes, 46–48
　baby Earth Dragons, 44–45
　coloring, 40
　eating habits, 43, 44–45, 48
　mating, 42–43
　scales, 40, 48
　size, 40, 44
　social organization, 46–49
Eating habits, 34
　of Earth Dragons, 43, 44–45, 48
　of Fire Dragons, 62
　of Water Dragons, 50, 56, 58, 60
Eggs, 34, 42–43, 56, 66
Eglantine, 51, 121, 127
Eleanor of Aquitaine, 79, 106
Esling, Peter Karl van, 54
Eurybatus, 100–102
Evil, 15, 26, 74, 77, 89

Fafnir, 132
Fauna Secreta, 67
Favorites, 36–37, 49, 86–87
Fire, 40, 49, 62, 67, 68, 96, 112, 138
Fire Dragons, 62–67
　abodes, 66
　coloring, 62, 66, 67
　eating habits, 62
　mating, 62
　scales, 62, 66
　social organization, 66, 67
Flying, 24, 40, 50, 67
　mating flights, 35, 42–43

Golden Apples, The, 94–95
Golden Dragon, The, 68–69
Golden Fleece, The, 96–97
Griselda, 106
Great Dragon, The, 88–89
Guardian Knight, 69

Hades, 92, 102
Hercules, 92, 94–95
Heritage, 88–89
Hermes, 92, 96

Hesperides, The, 94–95
Historia Naturalis, 23
Holy Grail, 69
Human forms (*See* "Disguises and illusory forms")
Humans, 20–21, 22, 37, 48–49, 56–57, 60, 66, 69, 74, 76, 82, 84–85, 86

Ichneumon, 23
Illness, 22–23, 27, 29
Inheritance, 40, 88
Isolde, 112–114

Jason, 96–97
Jewels, 20, 27, 45, 49, 86–87
Jilocasin, 78–79, 109–110
Jupiter, 94 (*See also* "Zeus")

Keeper, the, 69
Knights, 15, 68–69, 78–79
    in legends, 104, 106, 110, 112–114, 117–118, 120, 124, 127, 131

Lapis draconiensis aurulucentis, 88
Latin, 23, 45, 67
La Vibria, 122–124
Little Fire Dragons, 66–67
Lord of the Dragon, 85

Magic, 21, 32, 45, 60, 74, 85, 89, 138
    (*See also* "Black magic")
Magicians, 35, 58, 85
Mating, 32, 35, 36
    for Earth Dragons, 42–43
    for Fire Dragons, 62
    for Water Dragons, 56
Medea, 96–97
Medusa, 92
Melusine, 104
Merlin, 85
Music, 37, 49, 76–77, 121

Names, 21, 29, 32, 45, 124
Nature, 23, 74, 85, 88–89

Pages, 32, 40, 45, 46, 60
Perseus, 92
Physiology, 22–23
Pirofagus Reptilis Catalanae, 67
Pliny, 23
Poetry, 45, 50, 60, 69, 78–81, 106, 109
Poseidon, 92

Power stations, 66–67
Psychological characteristics, 20–21

Queens, 32, 66

Riddles, 20, 84–85

Sacred Chalice, 69
Saint Martha, 120–121
Scale corrosion, 22, 62
Scales, 23, 27–28, 29
    of Earth Dragons, 40, 48
    of Fire Dragons, 62, 66
    of the Golden Dragon, 68
    of Water Dragons, 54
Senile dementia, 22–23, 48–49
Servants, 26, 30, 37, 46, 48–49, 60, 62
Shining World, 88–89
Siegfried, 132
Sir Galahad, 69
Size
    of Earth Dragons, 40, 44
    of Little Fire Dragons, 66
    of Water Dragons, 54, 58
Skeleton, 24–25
Social organization, 36
    of Earth Dragons, 46–49
    of Fire Dragons, 66, 67
Sulfur, 66, 67
Sybaris of Cirfis, 100–102

Tannin, 128–129
Tarasque, The, 120–121
Treasure, 20, 26, 30, 46, 86–87, 118–119, 132
Tristan, 112–114

Virgins, 50, 58, 120, 125–126
Volcanoes, 62

Water Dragons, 50–60
    abodes, 60
    coloring, 50, 58
    eating habits, 50, 56, 58, 60
    mating, 56
    scales, 54
    size, 54, 58
Wings, 22, 24, 40, 42–43, 44–45, 68
Wing sacs, 35, 44
Worms of the deep, 22
Wort, Sir Reginald, 56

Zeus, 92, 98 (*See also* "Jupiter")

ciruelo